WISDOMS FROM BIG MOMMA'S PORCH

WISDOMS FROM BIG MOMMA'S PORCH

(Volume I)

Tammy Loraine Crowder

Writers Club Press
San Jose New York Lincoln Shanghai

Wisdoms from Big Momma's Porch
(Volume I)

All Rights Reserved © 2002 by Tammy Loraine Crowder

No part of this book may be reproduced or transmitted in any form or by any means, graphic, electronic, or mechanical, including photocopying, recording, taping, or by any information storage retrieval system, without the permission in writing from the publisher.

Writers Club Press
an imprint of iUniverse, Inc.

For information address:
iUniverse, Inc.
5220 S. 16th St., Suite 200
Lincoln, NE 68512
www.iuniverse.com

ISBN: 0-595-23379-1

Printed in the United States of America

To my sons Bryson and Seth

"The need for wisdom is spoken from the word at heart which puts us in harmony for the endurance of life."
—(Annie Lee Chatman aka Big Momma)

Contents

Foreword .... *xi*
Preface .... *xiii*

Personal Journeys
Inner Peace 3
A Short Story 7
So Deep but Dark 11
Bright Circle 15
Sunday Afternoon 17
He Watches over Me 21
The Writing Project 25
Wind Passion 29

Our Neighbors
Luther and the Cat 35
The Man in the Wheelchair 39
The Blind Lady 41
Young Girl 43
The Farmer and his Garden 47

The Family
Trouble in the Forest 53

Whipping Conscience 57
The Brown Bag. 61

Spirits/Supernatural
The Paintbrush. 75
A Childhood Memory 83
The Straw Hat. 87
Someone Called 89
Four O'clock. 91

A Fearful Night's Journey
The Origin of Departure 99
The Interstate 107
Destination 111
About the Author *121*

Foreword

"Entertaining and grasps your attention. It keeps you focused on the story that you are reading"

—Steve G. Johnson

"Tammy's book brought back memories of the times I spent with my own grandmother. Several of the stories in her book had me so captivated; it was hard to put it down. I wish her and the book great success and God Speed!"

—Lisha Jefferies

"Most people fail to find peace and happiness. They spend a lifetime trying to find who they are or where they are going. But that need not be true in your case. The experiences of people around the globe prove that contentment and a rewarding life are within your reach."
The author of this book has found something more valuable than gold and silver; and that is Wisdom from Big Momma's Porch and more importantly wisdom from God. This is what makes one find peace and happiness.

—Alvin Parson

Preface

Wisdoms from Big Momma's Porch are a collection of short stories. These stories are based on individuals (fiction and nonfiction), our imaginations, and the subconscious thoughts of the minds such as dreams and fantasies. But it's the setting of these stories that puts everything into perspective. You know the country, good o' pastimes while sitting on Big Momma's porch are recreated and recovered through these stories. These stories bring about a meaning because they consume the interest of the listeners as they discussed each one in detail. The depth of the stories is the underlying message of wisdoms that are derived in the conclusions. Examples: Personal Journeys is about struggles, endurance, and the search for peace, but how are these obtained? Spirits/supernatural: depicts how silly our imaginations are when they run wild, but in turn we recognize that we have an imagination and it's okay to have an imagination. *Wisdoms from Big Momma's Porch* display an array of emotions, but most of all it is a delightful book for the entire family to read. Remember just reading a simple book can constitute wisdom!

Tammy L. Crowder

Acknowledgements

"I would like to express my greatest appreciation to some special people Hazel, Barbara, Dorothy Rivers, Uncle Larnell, Mary Ann Polk, Lisha Jefferies, and Rev. Blalock for giving me the motivational drive to push me to continue to fulfill my dreams of getting my book published. You helped me to spiritually stay focused and you believed in me, and that means a lot."

Personal Journeys

Inner Peace

When my sister and I were very young, we would spend every summer with our Grandma Annie. Grandma Annie was a very busy and, and wise little old lady, but never too busy for my sister and me. By no means at all was she boring. She was as fiery as any wild creature and full of life. I was intrigued to be associated with someone that was so well rounded.

Grandma Annie was not your typical modern day woman. She used a metal scrub board and an old black pot to wash her clothes. Those clothes turn out so pretty and white. She had her own garden. Whatever she grew from the garden, she would can or freeze. She had all kinds of preserves, jams and jellies. Everything always smelled and tasted so delicious!

After we all had done a day's work, we would gather to sit on the porch. We watched the wind make dust funnels in the yard as it gathered up leaves, and the setting of the golden sun in the Far West.

"It sure feels good to let your mind be at ease and breath sometimes. It ain't good to keep your mind bottled up with a lot of confusion and junk. We need to learn to have an open mind. Just like we want our bodies to relax and relate so should our minds. "Learn to listen to our inner thoughts," stated Grandma Annie, as she steadily rocked back and forth in her rocking chair on the porch.

I was only eleven years old then, and I had no earthly idea of what Grandma Annie was talking about until 20 years later.

❦   ❦   ❦

I remember sitting in the living room on a cold wintry Sunday afternoon it was about one o'clock. During that time, the whole world seemed peaceful and still. I gazed out the window to see that the snow had covered the entire ground. The snow was about one feet or possibly two feet on the ground. Hanging from the icy trees on each branch and limb were crystal clear icicles that seem to sparkle as a hint of wind of passed near them. There was no sun just cloudiness and the air was still. The world is white! The only colors to be seen were a few red birds and blackbirds that manage to find a morsel of food in the blanket of snow. Two red deer were leaping across the road. To me this was peace, a time of reflection. Neither the phone nor the television disturbed me. The only thing I was interested in on TV was an old classic movie.

I stepped outside onto the back porch. I watch the birds gathered their food and then fly away. I shivered at the instant contact of a cold breeze that brushed my face. In a distance I could hear crackling and popping noises. It's probably frozen rotten branches falling from trees or squirrels scrounging for food. I gathered several sticks of wood for the heater and moved back into the house. I put as much wood as I possibly could into the heater. The warmth of the fire felt so wonderful! It made me thankful for being on the inside instead of being exposed to the cold. The house is at peace. Everyone is quietly asleep for a late afternoon nap. I too shall retire for a short afternoon nap.

❦   ❦   ❦

It has been very hot all day long. August seems like the hottest time of the year. The winds are blowing with great fury. It felt fantastic! I love this breath of fresh air that comes before a summer storm. The trees are dancing and so am I. I sit down on the porch to watch the clouds change from white to dark gray. I didn't want to move. I wanted to absorb as much of this wonderful breeze as I possibly could. I could foresee a bad storm coming. All of a sudden it's quiet, no wind stirring, no trees dancing, no birds flying, or anything moving. The clouds grew darker, but I continued to sit on the porch. I could smell the rain coming. I felt a drop on my leg. More drops came. They turned into an hundred drops then into sprinkles then into rain. I finally had to go into the house to be with the rest of the family. The rain felt so good, but I was getting too wet. Bright streaks of lightning flashed across the blackened sky. In a distance loud cracking and popping could be heard. The thunder roared and exploded endlessly making the world jump at each boom.

"Quickly, turn out all the lights and unplug the TV," shouted mother. "Hush, the Good Lord is working and you must be still."

We could not move about in the house. There had to be absolutely no noise. We all were calm and quiet.

I felt ridiculous at first, but it was wonderful to sit patiently to watch the lightning and thunder. It was wonderful to listen to the Good Lord as he talked to us through the thundering and lightning and the rain that fell on the tin roof. I could hear, smell, taste, see, and feel all what the Lord was saying. He spoke not one word but his presence was there. Isn't it good just to sit, relax, to think and to listen, listen and listen…?

I strolled into my neighbor's flower garden. I placed a quilted blanket on the freshly cut green lawn. I could see that she had flowers all lined up so beautifully in neat rows. I watched a yellow butterfly travel from one flower to another. A bumblebee chased it away so it could gather the nectar. I saw ants marching in a row like soldiers carrying bits of food to the big hole in the ground. All the insects seemed so busy; yet they get along so well. Just watching those insects made me be at peace with myself. Whatever I was upset about before has left my mind completely. This is the kind of therapy I like. I didn't have to pay a dime, use the phone or talk to anyone.

I believe I know what Grandma Annie was talking about now. Just reflecting back on those times taught me something. It taught me to slow down, take it easy and learn to listen from within; these things are priceless and will give you inner peace.

A Short Story

My mother and I did not have the best mother and daughter relationship. I often wondered was it because I was her stepchild, or was it because she may have felt second place to me since I was the child of the first wife that died? (This almost sounds like the story of Snow White and the wicked stepmother.) My stepmother was not wicked, but she treated me quite differently.

By the time I was two years old, the Good Lord blessed the union of my father and stepmother with a child, a little girl. If my memory serves me correctly, my sister and I got along well during our early childhood years. But as the years progressed, my sister and I developed a relationship that sort of turned sour. My sister had adopted a spirit of meanness that only Satan himself could identify with. She was hateful, spoiled, and downright lowdown at times. She always got her way because she was sly and cunning.

I on the other hand, received the majority of the punishments just because of my stepsister. In my mind I was thinking I could really hurt her, but I knew what consequences would develop, so I let the matter dissolve from my mind.

I never will forget the time we were preparing to go to Sunday morning worship. My sister and I were dressed like little darling angels waiting on the front porch until our parents were dressed. That little devil of a sister of mine sneaked up behind me while I stood at the edge of the porch. I never anticipated on her doing anything sneaky since we were dressed for church, but boy was I wrong.

Unexpectedly I discovered I was falling toward the ground to land in the dirt and dust. My sister had pushed me off the porch. When I angrily looked up at her, she cupped her hand over her mouth as if she had not done a thing. I screamed. My stepmother came running to the front door. She knew what had taken place, but kept mum. It was obvious she did not want daddy to find out. But I blurted out; "She pushed me off the porch."

I could hear daddy rushing to the front door. He stood at the threshold of the front door and peeking out saying, "Tam what happened to you?"

I explained to him that dear old stepsister had pushed me off the porch and made me get my clothes dirty. Daddy was furious. Instantly, he demanded that I come into the house and change my clothes. At that point he stepped outside onto the porch and began to whip my stepsister. My stepmother could not bear the sight of my sister getting a whipping so she hurriedly entered into the house.

Situations seem to get worse as we grew older. If my mother had to hand anything to me, or collect anything she would thrust it at me or snatch it. I felt like an orphan or an animal. I felt as if I was in the way, but my dad was there. It wasn't so much of what he said to control the situations, but to know of his presence. This always boosted my self-esteem. And it made me stronger. If my father was not present, I could always count on my Big Momma. She never sided, but always gave me comfort.

I remember in Grammar school three of my girlfriends were discussing the golden rules set forth by their mothers on staying clean. One of the girls said that her mother would have a fit if she got her new white blouse dirty. And another said that her mother ordered her not to get dirt on her clothes at all. I had nothing to say. I had no golden rule etiquettes of cleaning to contribute to this conversation. So I felt awkward and out of place. But I casually acted nonchalantly about the whole situation. I started wondering in my mind, "Why haven't my mother made a fuss over my clothes? Did she care?" My conclusion was she did not care.

That very evening when I arrived home, I asked my mother why she doesn't concern herself with teaching me how to be prim and proper. My mother's reply, "She did not know," And politely walked away.

The bus was on its way to pick me for school that morning. I don't know what the problem was, but my stepmother forgot to comb my hair. I walked about the house with my hair sticking all over my head. That same morning our neighbor was visiting us. My stepmother and the neighbor became so engaged in a conversation, it was like I was invisible. I did not want to be rude, but I had to remind my stepmother about my uncombed head. Why did I do that? She went in search of a comb, and came back with an awful mean look on her face. I did not like that look. By this time I became scared and had changed my mind about getting my hair combed.

She jerked, twisted, and pulled my head like she was wringing clothes from washing. My head and feelings were hurt. I was glad when she finished combing my hair. I had one big puffball standing on top of my head. I ran out the door with tears in my eyes. I was praying the other children did not poke fun of my puffball hairdo. Next time I will comb my own hair.

My mother never had patience with me. Any patience she had she utilized it all on my stepsister. She should have had some kind of patience with me since I was the oldest. For example, I had the mistaken privilege of asking my mother about the facts of life. My mother acknowledges me by saying that if I got pregnant she would knock the baby out of me. And that was the end of that conversation. How can someone be so unconcerned and inconsiderate? It was like talking to a plant and waiting for it to respond back to you. I needed my Big Momma.

All I wanted was to have a mother that loved me, and not to be pushed away. But thank God for my Big Momma (grandmother).

She was able to fill the voids that my stepmother couldn't and wouldn't fill. My prayer is whenever the Good Lord blesses me with children whether they are my own, my stepchildren, or the combination of both that I treat them all equal with a loving kind heart. I pray that he gives me the good sense to ask for knowledge and wisdom on how to raise my children. And to be there when they need me.

So Deep but Dark

The phone rings and its Friday 11:30p.m. It's my husband Lee on the other end calling me to pick him up. Lee is a sick and pathetic person. He needs help, but refuses it. He has been in and out of all types of treatment centers.

I'm surprised he is not harassing me for more money. That really annoys me when he calls all times of the night begging for money. When he starts begging, I just hang up the phone. I do not want to hear all that nagging and whining. Majority of the time we have the money, but I have to constantly lie saying, "There is no money." I was beginning to feel like I was lying as much as he was.

Our little funds had to last until my next payday. You hear me, my next payday. He doesn't have a payday. He can't keep a job long enough to establish anything. Lee tries to threaten and scare me into giving him money, but I am used to his tactics. If he doesn't receive any money after all his 'air-puffing' then he resorts to physical abuse by pushing and slapping me around. I stand up to his big 6'1", 280 pounds stature. I am tired and fed up with that damn Lee. I am going to find a way to get out of this forsaken marriage.

I dressed the baby and we proceeded to go pick up Lee. When we arrive, Lee is not quite ready to go. He wants to stay, but he needs money. That maniac does this to me every time! Pretending he is ready to come home but changes his mind to stay when he sees me. It's a trick just to get money. How manipulative and no consideration. Doesn't he know I have to get both the baby and myself out of bed? Then get dressed and warm up the car? And then proceed to pick him up at his present point of destination (wherever that may be). Or perhaps go search for him if he is nowhere to be found.

    I fooled him this time; I did not bring any money. He already had $150.00 earlier tonight. Where is that? Apparently, he spent the money on drugs. No I am not happy to see him. Sometimes the scene gets real ugly. After screaming, yelling, and arguing, I am ready to go home. He curses me because I will not let him have the car. Then he's going to pester me all night long by calling all times of the night begging me to pick him up. Why should I bother to pick him up at all, when I know what he is capable of? He is clever, convincing, and conniving. Usually, I believe him and fall for his lies. That's how simple it was. Well, not tonight, and not any more. I'm tired. I told Lee I was going home and would not be returning. He can walk home or stay out all night. I did not care any more. As I left in a steamy rage, the rubber on the tires squalled on the asphalt. I needed to get my child back home safely in bed.

    As soon as I stepped into my house, I immediately unplugged the phone. I refuse to hear that phone ringing again all night long. Then I thought what if something happens; and he can't get through to me? Nonchalantly, I figured, if it hasn't happen by now; it probably won't. Besides when he gets money, I never see him for several days. So what's the difference? No need to keep my nerves worked up.

    I want this man out of my life. I want him GONE! Years have been wasted because I allow myself to put up with his sorry butt I supported, stood-by, listened, watched, waited, try to understand, gave up some things, almost lost my job, (and the list goes on), for this man. And I am still in the same rut. My life is at a standstill, but with the help of the good Lord, things are going to get better. And they are going to be good.

    For now I have to deal with the situation at hand. I think I will pack up and leave. No, why should I leave? I found this apartment. Lee needs to leave. Fear is causing me to wonder and doubt. Can I handle the rent and other bills by myself? How will I make it? It's going to be hard, but I am going to strive and survive.

One of these days I am secretively going to buy a house for my son and myself. When Lee comes back home from his 'got-to-be-gone-spree', he will not find us. This house will be empty. We will be gone! Won't he be surprised?

Bright Circle

I sat on the floor in the living room gazing out an open window. Through the open window I felt the stormy breeze that was blowing. I was deep in thought. Then I started to pray.

When I prayed, I noticed the Lord was busy at work. The winds were blowing heavily and the lighting flashed across the sky. The trees moved in rhythm with each breath of wind that the Lord was blowing.

I ceased praying to look at the clouds. I noticed an unusual bright circle among the darkness in the sky. In that circle a form or a shape of something was taking place. It looked to be one of God's angels ascending into the brightness of the circle; and heaven was stretched out in the background. I recalled asking the Lord, "Is that one of your angels?"

I remember telling myself, "No that was not an angel, only a symbol." It symbolized truth and hope. I noticed the circle got larger and larger. I wanted to cry. My eyes swelled with tears. It was like God was communicating to me through this circle of brightness. It's going to be okay. I felt relieved, over whelmed, full of joy then I smiled, because I was heavily burdened.

I searched above to make sure there were no other circles of brightness in the sky. This could have been a coincidence. No, it wasn't. I saw no other places in the sky that resembled this circle. Then the circle of brightness slowly faded away into the night sky.

Sunday Afternoon

One Sunday afternoon I sat on the porch watching the traffic zip and zoom up and down the streets. I was in the mood for writing, but could not think of one particular topic I wanted to write about. My mind was like a wheel spinning excessively out of control. So while I sit contemplating on a topic, I enjoyed the cool summer breeze that breathed across the porch onto my heat-exhausted body.

My six-year-old son Tyson was running back and forth into the house trying to find the perfect toy to play with. In the midst of all this, he did find some red ants on the ground to stomp on.

At this moment, I realized this was a time to relax and reflect. Oh how we often take so much for granted in our lives. Unaware or not realizing that some of the best times or best things in our lives are the simple things. We complicate our own lives.

Time after time I pondered on the idea of what my life would have been like if I had not married. Don't get me wrong. I love the idea of being married, but my marriage was not one of those made in heaven. A lesson learned. My attempts to make a success of our marriage became a handicap because only I made the effort to work at the marriage. A one sided marriage is too much work for one person, so my efforts were in vain.

Those countless nights of being alone, there was no acknowledgement, gratification, or kind words expressed during holidays, anniversaries, and special occasions. So I became very bitter. Engaging in a mere conversation with my friends or overhearing conversations of how wonderful other husbands were made me envy with jealousy. They would express how their husbands spoiled and loved them; and I on the other hand would be hurting and crying on the inside.

To make my husband look good, I pretended he was going to do all these wonderful things for me. Or I would say he is out of town on a big job making money for me. In reality, he would be at home lounging on the couch contemplating ideas of how he was going to swindle money out of me. Sometimes I never knew where he was; he would be gone for days.

Constant bickering and arguing went on all the time. For nine years I dealt with this mess. I finally had to call it quits. He objected to me pulling out of the marriage, but it was something I had to do. I took the initiative to do things for myself and by myself. I did not need him. Why? He was a hindrance and he was never around.

For me, love is a closed subject. It has been far too many years since a man has swept me off my feet. I don't think I could be persuaded. I'm afraid of being hurt. I learn to live with the fact that for me love is not destined. Keeping my options open is not a question of consideration; it's not even a question to be acknowledged.

Spiritually, I have two principals of strengths that keep me going. One is God and the other is my son. Without these two I would be like a car without a driver. I would be steered, but in what direction? That's what God and my son does for me, they keep me focus and help me to steer for the right direction. I asked the Good Lord to help me in my trials and tribulations. My inner strength overpowers the depression and loneliness. God gives me physical strength, and my son gives me joy! So therefore, one plus one equals two powers of greatness to keep me running on full.

I don't want my son to follow in the footsteps of his father. I want him to be a wise and perceptive individual. It's up to me to make the effort to mold and shape my precious son. I ask for wisdom and knowledge to help me to be the best mother I can be for my son. It's hard, but I am willing and determined. I will succeed.

I like to know my son's opinion on certain things so I ask him for his input. He doesn't hesitate to explain what's on his mind. And I like that. He elaborates and I learn to listen to a child's point of view.

I'm still trying to find a topic to write on; I seem to have developed writer's block. I became distracted by the activities that were around me as I continued to sit on the porch. I could hear the lonesome sound of an airplane taking flight in the sky. In a distance I could hear the roaring noises of vehicles rolling swiftly on the expressway. Two black birds were engaged in a playful game of chase while flying in the air.

My son and the neighbor's child are playing. They use vivid imagination in their wild games of play. Their laughter represents happiness. No need for worries from these young and energetic minds. These are the simple and small things of life, and we never want to take these things for granted! I'm thankful for my simple moments. They leave a lasting smile upon my face. That's why Sunday afternoons can be as simple as—well, I've told you mine, you go find your own.

He Watches over Me

Tonight I had anticipated on returning to work to do some overtime after hours. When I arrived home, I discovered that my utilities had been disconnected. This put a damper on my plans to do any kind of overtime. I had planned on picking up the kids, purchasing some Chinese for dinner, and returning to work. Instantly my plans were shattered and I needed to take care of my business at home.

Well, I guess the good Lord had other plans for me so it seems. It was the middle of summer and I did not want to be uncomfortable in my own house without some form of cooling system.

My oldest son discovered the disconnection notice hanging on the front door. He knew what that meant. It was like déjà vu, a flashback, going down memory lane for him. He has experienced this frightful event before. When he was only four years old, he and I remember coming home to find the utilities off, no heat, and no food in the refrigerator. We were devastated! That was one horrible and uncomfortable experience that left a lasting effect on my son. I promised him that that would never happen again—but it did. I felt bad.

"Look mom," he shouted. "This was hanging on the door. Are our lights off?"

I said nothing. I looked away in disgust. My upset son had a perplexing look upon his face. It was like he wanted to lash out at me for being irresponsible. I explained to him sometimes my money is short and I have to pay what I can on the bills. But I was puzzled also.

I had another week before the bill was due; so why are my utilities being disconnected a week early? I couldn't and didn't understand. I just said, "Thank you Jesus for blessing us."

My oldest son starred at me. He couldn't understand why I was given thanks for having the utilities turned off. He said, "I don't see how you consider this a blessing, because I don't. As a matter of fact it is not good."

I couldn't quite put my finger on it, but I knew some good would come out of this. Maybe I was happy because it wasn't raining, snowing, or that the weather was not freezing cold. I couldn't give him a straight answer at the time, but I still felt like this was the opportune time to be thankful.

The issue of overtime crossed my mind again. By this time I did not care if I had overtime or not. I already had some overtime from the previous days. We took the night off just to be a family at home.

It occurred to me that today is Wednesday. It is Bible Study time. I had already told the Reverend that I would not be attending Bible Study because I had to work. "I know the Lord is punishing me because I did not go to Bible Study," I said to myself.

In my heart I knew this was not the case. There is another reason why I got sidetrack from doing some overtime and having my utilities disconnected. I couldn't quite put my finger on it, but something is stirring in the air.

My sixth sense kicked in. I had this eerie feeling two of my co-workers, my supervisor, and ex-executive secretary were up to something suspicious and sneaky. I noticed at 5:30 p.m. that the four of them had not left for the day. What were they up to? Whatever it was, I wanted no part of their low-down, underhanded, and conniving devilish games. I don't trust them. If that meant no overtime for today, so be it.

While my wheels were spinning in my head, I had already made my arrival at the utility department, paid my due balance, and was returning home to wait for them to restore my utilities. We waited outside on the porch. Thank God for daylight saving time! In a matter of 30 minutes our services were restored.

Thursday morning I arrived to work 30 minutes early. I wanted to get in some overtime. I noticed the ex-executive secretary had arrived early also. I laughed to myself when I saw her.

"These people think they are fooling me. I know exactly what they are up to now," I said to myself.

My hunch was right. They were spying on me to see if I was really working or goofing off. They were going to spy on me yesterday had I worked overtime. I received word through the grapevine confirming that is exactly what they were up to. Those are some old sneaky heifers.

They got fooled yesterday. They did not get to spy on me. They could not watch me. Now I know. That's why my utilities were disconnected. God did not want me in the midst of their dirty work. He knew they meant trouble. He intervened in their plans and made it be meant for my good. So my "thank you Jesus" was never said in vain.

This little incident lets me know that God has already taken control of the situation. Everything happens for a reason. Every eventful situation that occurred, there was a blessing that occurred also. You know, I know the Lord watches over me.

Thank you!

The Writing Project

I procrastinated about a writing project that I just couldn't or maybe didn't want to start. At the same time every morning at 3:00 or 4:00 a.m., I would wake up thinking about this writing project. I knew it was the good Lord trying to motivate me to get up and work on that project. I could not bring myself to get out of that bed. I wanted to be lazy. So I lie there wrestling with the thought of whether or not I wanted to raise out of bed. I chose not to. Perhaps it was because I knew I had to be at work and needed the extra time for more sleep. Well, the weekends weren't any better. I refused to get up because I didn't have to work. I needed my rest.

What makes it so bad; I would sincerely pray my little heart out asking the good Lord to help me with this writing project. I would ask for guidance, knowledge, and wisdom. In the meantime, what effort of energy had I contributed to this great writing project that I prayed, begged, and pleaded about? None, I had not done one thing, absolutely no accomplishments at all. That's how we do. And once again another day has gone by and I have not exerted myself to achieve anything.

Upon rising this one particular Saturday morning, I was compelled to work on my writing project. First I procrastinated, and then hesitated, then I persuaded myself to become productive. Yeah right! I decided to do all my personal errands very early that morning.

Then afterwards when I return home, I would totally commit myself to my great writing project. All my errands were done in a timely manner. It felt good to be home by 12:00 noon.

I was eager and excited to get started on my great writing project. I actually turned on the switch to the computer. But then something unexpectedly happened. The computer made no sound. There was no flashing green lights, buzzing, startup sounds, or a lit monitor screen. The computer appeared to be dead. But it can't be happening now. I needed this time to work on my great writing project. I remained calm trying to think this situation through. So I immediately turned off the computer and turned it back on. The same thing happened again. The computer did nothing. The monitor was still black. There weren't any pictures, sounds, or anything. I tackled the printer and the speakers to see if they would work. They were dead also. There seemed to be a malfunction in the whole computer system. I could not find a justifiable reason why the system would be dead. I was doomed and so was my great writing project. I wiggled, twisted, pulled, and tugged the wires to make sure that they were properly connected. I tried the switch again. Silence was all I heard.

By now I was almost hyperventilating and panicking. I almost convinced myself in believing I needed a new computer. That meant I needed money, to check prices, and the endless search of where to purchase a new or used computer. It was in my best interest to continue tampering with this computer until I could get it working.

I began to pray to myself. I remember saying, "Lord if and when I get this computer working again, I was going to work on my project until it is completed. I was not going to stop, talk on the telephone, or take a break for any reason at all."

When I finished praying, I analyzed every square inch of that computer trying to determine the sudden breakdown. I shook my head in dismay and sat on the floor starring at the computer. I finally came to grips that I needed to psyche and prepare myself into purchasing a new computer.

Suddenly without cause, something amazing happened. The computer started up. I could see the little green lights flashing, and flickering. I could hear the buzzing and humming of the startup inside the computer. I saw a beautiful light on the monitor screen. The printer chattered and tapped as the speakers blasted tremendous loud sounds. I leaped for joy! And my eyes flashed with excitement. My computer was up and ready.

I wasted no time in succeeding to finish my great writing project. I gathered all I needed and commence to typing at once. I was determined to complete this project. I was not going to let anything hinder me. But you know the devil is busy.

The phone would ring. I tried to ignore it. I would say, "Devil please leave me alone. I am going to finish this project. I will not talk on the phone." I thought the kids would annoy me, but they were good. I had no trouble out of them. They were asleep.

I applied myself diligently to finish this great writing project. At approximately 5:00 p.m., the project was perfected and corrected to completion. Hats off to me!

I presumed the Lord was trying to tell me something, or to say, "I'll show you." I don't think the Lord likes the idea of us asking for things and we aren't ready to receive it, or put any effort on our part to get something done. In other words God helps those who helps themselves. The Lord knows I wasn't helping myself. I prayed, procrastinated, and eventually did not care. That's why my computer went on the blinks. I almost did not have the opportunity to complete my project. This was a close call. I learned my lesson. And you know he got my attention real good.

The End

Wind Passion

As I became older, so did my quest for love and affection. I have a longing desire for that gentle touch of his hand caressing my body. My yearning is so strong that I can almost already feel the touches. I believe in its presence because I smell it and feel it. And in my mind I want it.

Love can be an everlasting thing. It should be invigorating, yet so stimulating! It should exist indefinitely like the continuous winds that blow from the four-corners of the world. I am blown away into passion by this breathtaking experience. It's the ultimate!

I stood on the back porch late one summer afternoon freshly bathed, barefooted, and cocoon in a white beach towel. That towel draped around my shoulders exposing my chest and the top part of my tender brown breasts. I wanted to feel as relaxed as I possible could, and I did. I leaned against the white column holding up the porch so that I could inhale some fresh air. I breathed deeply as I closed my eyes so that I could feel the rush of air racing through my nostrils to circulate throughout the veins and arteries in my body.

"That was refreshing!" I told myself.

Suddenly, the wind gently grabbed hold of my toes and slowly caressed its way up my legs, waist, back, neck, and then finally my head. It had me. It was embracing me. When it reached my head I became dizzy. I was lightheaded with excitement and numbness! All my familiar surroundings seem to fade away. My mind became a blank. My body perspired with wetness. And at any given time, I knew I was going to explode with intense excitement. By now it was dark and the moon was shining and I danced naked in the shimmering glow of the moonlight.

The wind suddenly left as quickly as it came. I did not feel the wind blowing so I knew it had finally stopped stirring. At least that's what I thought. The moment I sat down on the porch, I heard the wind stirring, when before I felt it. It was racing through the trees. It was trying to acquaint itself with each and every leaf on the trees, (like a man does when he meets a group of women).

Finally the wind breathed on me. This time there was something different about the wind. The velocity was much greater but gentler. The wind whispered in my ears. It tickled, but I wanted to hear more. I did not move. I let that wind talk to me because I loved what it was saying. It was like a man whispering sweet nothings in my ear. I smiled, laughed and giggled the whole time. My eyes were closed tight. My nose sensed a strange aroma in the air. It smelled like sweetness of honeysuckle flowers after a summer rain. Then it smelled of sweetness like snow melting off the mountaintop that turned into clear water running down a hilly mountainside into a fertile green valley. The aroma became stronger and stronger with each motion of the wind. Then I knew—it smelled of a man! During all of this my eyes remained closed. This was so indescribable!

I was being whisked away. I could feel myself perspiring again. Moisture saturated my entire body. My nipples became hardened as I yearned for that lustful affection. I recognized a wonderful sensation that was arousing and it transmuted me into exhilarating euphoria! The wind has positioned me to be more in tone with the nature of a spirited inner soul. I had the natural ability that I can enjoy this and absorb all the pulsating moments of my erogenous zones; and I would not be disturbed or hindered by my surroundings. I am in my own world grasping the eternity wind of passion for the sake of feeling loved. By whom, who knows? I know this was a momentary thing for my imagination to run wild and for my time to be pampered, but by whom? It doesn't matter. I just knew I liked what I was experiencing.

The wind continued to caress and embrace my body as the turbulence of passion stirred inside of me. And I knew this was not of a dream because I lay covered with some leaves. Leaves blown by the wind of passion to shield my nakedness, as I lay on the white beach towel in the shimmering moonlight.

Our Neighbors

Luther and the Cat

There was an elderly couple that resided on a farm at the edge of Turner Town. The couple was well known as Big Daddy and Big Momma by the townspeople. Their real names were Luther and Annie. Luther or Big Daddy had to be the scariest man in town. He reminded you so much of Barney Fife of the Andy Griffith Show. He was a thin man that spoke very little. Annie, on the other hand, always did a great deal of talking. She never met a stranger.

It was the dead of winter and freezing cold outside. It was so cold your nose would get frostbitten the second it bypassed the threshold of the door. Big Daddy and Big Momma went to bed exactly at 8:00 p.m. every night. They rarely watched TV.

One night while they were in bed, the wind began to howl and blow fiercely. Anything that could be moved by the wind would swirl and twirl wildly in the air until it banged or smashed against the house. The wind blew so hard it sounded like a melody being played because of its long enchanting whistle.

Big Momma thought she heard a cow outside on the front porch. She heard it moo several times, but could not determine the direction of the noise. She heard it again. At the same time, she heard a bumping noise against the side of the house. She feared the cow was wandering loose and dropping cow patties on the front porch and the yard.

"Luther," Big Momma shouted, "get up and see what is making that bumping noise on the outside of the house and also check to see if the cow is wondering loose."

Big Daddy just lay there. His little pea head was already covered up from being so frightened, or maybe he never heard the noises. Big Momma hunched him under the covers. He raised his head to look at Big Momma, and finally said.

"Why don't you get up and check? You are the one that heard the noise. I did not hear anything."

About that time there was another bumping noise against the side of the house.

"Can't you hear that?" asked Big Momma.

"Hear what? No, I didn't hear anything."

Immediately, Big Daddy covered his head back up and pulled the covers tighter to his body.

"Get up Luther and stop acting scary," demanded Big Momma.

Big Daddy looked at Big Momma and gave her a hard look. He rolled his eyes and sighed real hard. He got up and very slowly moved toward the front door. Cautiously, he pulled open the door. It was opened just wide enough for Big Daddy to poke his head out. Very slowly and carefully he peeked out. As he opened the door, something fuzzy whizzed through the door and ran across his feet. It was a cat! Big Daddy instantly jumped into the air and quickly slammed the door shut. When he slammed that door, the tip of the cat's tail got smashed. The cat let out a loud squeaky and squalling meow, and it tried to fight Big Daddy. Big daddy on the other hand was ready to run and take flight!

"FEET TAKE CARE OF BODY AND DON'T FAIL ME NOW," he shouted.

So between that poor cat's frantic squeaking and squalling and Big Daddy's hollering, they frightened away the bumping noise that was going on outside. There was more commotion going on inside the house than outside. Big Daddy never found out what was making that bumping noise against the house. Big Momma looked at Big Daddy then shook her head. She lay back down. Finally, she grumbled out loud, "MEN you can't live without them but Lord knows I sure could tonight just so that I can get some sleep."

The Man in the Wheelchair

I met a man in a wheelchair. He told me that the wheelchair was his car. He had no use of his legs. His arms were strong, as iron and this was his source of power. He used the arms for the gas and accelerator. He had a strong navigated mind that kept him steered for effortless driving. His only companion was a black German shepherd that stayed by his side every mile he traveled.

The man was determined to travel the streets and roads. As sweat beamed above his brows, he would push and grunt as he climbed hills. He did not ask for help from anyone, but ask that people get out of his way. He could be seen almost anywhere traveling through town. He amazed me with his will power and determination to go on. His mind set on 'GO'. There is no stopping for the man in the wheelchair.

And we complain because we have to walk across the street.

The Blind Lady

I stood in my yard one day watching my neighbor from a distance. She was standing on her bedroom balcony soaking up the sun. She sat down in a chair and began to read a book. The next day I was in the yard refueling the lawnmower. I heard my neighbor call out from her balcony, "Oh what a beautiful day!"

"Yes it is," I replied. "It is gorgeous."

She left her balcony and I joined her on the porch. From that point on we talked and talked for several hours. I had forgotten that the yard still needed mowing. By now it was late in the evening.

She was petite and dressed so neatly. I could tell from our conversation that she was a very intelligent young lady. She spoke Spanish and French fluently. She talked like she had traveled the world. I especially liked her adventures she had in Africa. I listened tentatively as she spoke softly with great wisdom.

"You have a beautiful yard. Your flowers are as beautiful as the gardener."

"Thank you," I said with a smile.

"I love nature in the summertime. Can't you hear the birds singing and the bees buzzing? I even love the way the butterflies flutter around the flowers. The ants are the most exciting to watch. They travel like an army so busy at work!"

Then she told me she was blind. I was shocked, but amazed at this young lady.

"Don't be alarmed. I am still human," as she smiled and held my hand. "Don't take life for granted. To acquire knowledge one has to experience, sustain, and resolve to the realities that are offered by life."

I once was blind but now I see!

Young Girl

Growing up as a child, I was a little wild tomboy. Anything a boy could do, I could do better. When he climbed a tree, rode his bike, or run a relay race, I felt I could do better.

"Belinda, you better stop playing with those boys so much. Find some girls to play with," said momma.

All the kids in my neighborhood that were my age were boys. All my cousins that came over to visit were boys. My female cousins were either too old or too young. So I hung out with the boys.

The summer of 1988 I was 12 years old. I was too young to stay lady-like and too old for kiddy stuff. The five of us—Kevin, Ray, Craig, Winston, and myself found interesting stuff to do. Winston was the oldest he was 14 and the other boys were 13. They always looked after me like I was their baby sister. Wherever we went, they protected me.

Most of the time we played near Walter's Creek. This wasn't too far from where I lived. We lived on the outskirts of town. Going to the creek was like going to the country. It was a good thing I could swim. The boys were always throwing me in the water.

One particular day, I went looking for the boys and I could not find them. The only other place they could be was at the old clubhouse. This clubhouse used to be a garage. The boys had found the garage and cleaned it up. It still was in pretty good shape. It had a concrete floor and a loft in the top. I don't know why a loft would be in a garage?

I sneaked my way to the clubhouse trying to catch the boys doing something. It was so quiet. They were in the clubhouse. They heard me coming because they started moving around and talking loud. They ran out the door acting surprised to see me.

"Hi Belinda, what's up?" asked Craig.

"Nothing. What were you boys doing? Probably something bad I bet?" I replied.

"No we were just chilling out," explained Winston.

Of course I did not believe them. I knew they were up to something. That's okay. I'll find out later when they aren't around. They must have something in there they do not want me to see.

So we left together heading for Roy's Farm. This was Ray's grandfather. Mr. Roy had just received a new shipment of pigs and he wanted Ray to bring his friends to the farm to see the pigs. Mr. Roy had just unloaded the last pig when we arrived. Man those pigs were stinking!

I could not handle the smell. I stood back looking at the pigs from a distance. The boys seemed so interested in the pigs. You would have thought this was their first time seeing a group of pigs. They acted like I did not exist. So I left. I started for home then I got to thinking about the clubhouse. This was the opportune time for me to investigate the mystery the boys were being secretive about. I headed straight for the clubhouse.

I entered with caution; because knowing those boys they probably had booby traps all over the place. Finally, I was in. The boys had accumulated so much junk. Junk was everywhere stacked in several piles. I look through, over, and under all their junk. I didn't even know what I was looking for. I bumped into something, and accidentally knocked it over. It was a wooden board that served as a tabletop. The board rested on top of a crate. The board was covered with a light green cloth. I picked up the board to put it back on the crate. Low and behold, I found magazines inside the crate. Not just any old magazines, but I discovered they were *Playboy* magazines!

My mouth dropped open. The boys were looking at dirty magazines, and they were trying to hide these from me. There was a whole stack of them inside the crate. I glimpsed through a few of them. My eyes had seen enough.

"Oh my goodness, man look at that," was all I could say.

I thought for a moment, this is exactly the kind of stuff my mother had told me about. She said men like this kind of stuff. And boys would too if they were ever to read any of these kind of magazines. It only entices little boys to get into trouble. So be careful. I once heard my older sister Gina talking to her girlfriend about these magazines. I never knew what she was talking about because I never paid her any attention. Now I know!

Quickly, I put away the magazines and everything else exactly the way I found it. I swung open the clubhouse door preparing to make a mad dash for home, but I ran into Winston. I shrieked.

"Winston, you scared me."

"What's wrong Belinda? You look like you saw a ghost?"

"Ah nothing. I-I-I-I lost my, my ah birthstone ring my mother gave me. So I came looking for it."

Winston just stood there. He was giving me a look I had never seen before. It did not feel right. Chills went all over my body. I tried to walk away, but Winston stood in front of me. He moved closer to get right in my face. He forced me to back into a tree. Winston grabbed hold of my hand and kissed my forehead.

"Did you like what you saw in those magazines?" he whispered in my ear.

I gave him an angry look and slapped him. I ran away from Winston as fast as I could. I never looked back. The whole time I was running I kept hearing momma's voice telling me to be careful. I could still feel Winston's wet lips on my forehead. That was the very last time I hung out with the boys.

The Farmer and his Garden

One day a farmer rose early in the wee hours of the dawn to break ground in his back yard to start a garden. He wanted to get an early start. He did not want to be attacked by the intense heat of the hot sun. Then therefore, he would not be able to work productively.

He was busy tilling and plowing all morning long. By 12:00 noon, he stopped to take a lunch break. At 1:00, he was full, well rested, and ready to go back to work. Now of course, by this time of the day, the sun was beaming hot. He farmer didn't complain. He just wiped sweat from his forehead and continued his work. When he did speak up, he managed to say, "It is really hot out here. I don't know how much longer I can stand this hot sun."

He finished preparing the garden for sowing. At 6:00 p.m. he went in for the evening to rest up for the next day.

The farmer rose early the second day. He felt pretty good because he had achieved one goal—which was breaking the ground for gardening. Now he was ready to plant his seeds and other plants.

Like before he worked until lunch, then he took a lunch break. The sun was so humid by the time lunch was over, the farmer almost refused to finish the garden. He motivated himself into finishing up the garden. Once his garden starts producing, he will have those wonderful green, yellow, red, big, and delicious vegetables to eat. Still sweating and pushing himself to finish, he kept going until he fell down in the middle of the garden.

"Lord, this sun sure is hot. I wish it would just go away for a moment so I can finish my garden," said the farmer.

What the farmer did not realize is that instead of praying, he was complaining. At that very moment the sun went in and the skies became gray. Cool breezes start to blow. This made the farmer feel good. He knew now that he would be able to finish his garden without all the intense hot heat. He moved a little faster, thinking the sun may peek back out again from under the clouds.

Every day from then on the skies were always gray. There was no sun to be seen. The world was so dark and gloomy. Several weeks had passed since the farmer finished his garden. He would randomly check to see if there were any sprouts coming out of the ground. Nothing, absolutely nothing to be seen sprouting out of the ground. Then he became inpatient and started checking every day. He was getting upset.

"Why is this happening? I worked hard to put this garden together. I worked from sun up to sun down. And what do I have to show for all that work, nothing. I won't have any produce to put up for the winter for my family. What am I going to do?"

Every day he complained and the sun would stay hid behind the clouds. Before long the summer was almost gone, and the farmer still did not have a garden. Did he even realize what he had done? No, he was being selfish and wasn't thinking about anybody or anything else but himself. So every living plant as far as he could see—died.

Finally, one day he stepped outside and looked around. He noticed there was no 'green life' to be seen.

"Hmm," he said to himself. "Something does not look right. The sky is always gray and the trees and plants are almost dead. What has happened?"

Then it dawned on him. The day he was in his garden sowing seeds, he had prayed that the sun would go away. He was devastated.

He put his hands up side of his head and yelled as loud as he could. He started to cry.

"Look what I have done. I have destroyed everything around me. No life to be seen anywhere. Without the sun, there is no life. Plants and trees need chlorophyll to produce their green coloring and I have destroyed that. Oh Lord please, forgive me. I did not realize what I was saying. Please restore the sunshine so all the plants can be pretty, alive, and green again."

At that very moment, the sun gradually peeked out from the clouds bursting with rays of bright sunshine. The rays were so bright they almost blinded the farmer since his eyes had not seen sunlight in so long. The world seemed to smile! As if they had been in a deep sleep, one by one all living plants and trees started to blossom. The farmer could see plants sprouting in his garden. He smiled and cheered for joy! He would finally have a garden, but it would be a late garden, which was fine by him. He realizes that man needs to be careful for that which he prays for, for he may very well get what he asks for.

The next morning when he arose, he saw a beautiful green garden in full bloom.

"Now when my family and I eat, we thank God for every morsel of food that goes into our mouths and the sun that helps make them grow. Thank you dear Lord!"

The Family

Trouble in the Forest

They were one big happy family living at the edge of a heavily dense forest. One day in the early spring, a patch of wild thorny pink and red roses was stretching to the rising of the sun.

"Oh that sun is so beautiful. It has such a bright golden color," said one of the red roses.

Then one by one the remaining roses began to blossom. The roses felt vibrant and ecstatic to be alive. Their sweet aroma was released into the air as they gleamed in the sun.

A prickly and bushy little shrub was standing nearby. It shook itself real hard to get that final stretch. The leaves on the shrub clapped together and positioned themselves into place on the little shrub.

"Oh I feel good!" shouted the oak tree.

"So do we!" said the pine and the apple trees together.

The trees waved their leaves and they shook with joy.

"My head feels wonderful! It's just great to have a head full of leaves rather than be empty-headed. The wind may have trouble blowing through my leaves because they are so thick," laughed the apple tree.

They stood proudly and perky every day all spring long. The intense heat of the summer sun caused the plants to barely survive. Finally, autumn came.

"We barely survived the hot heat of the summer, and I must say we do look a mess. We are not beautiful anymore. Look at my fir," groaned the pine tree. "It's all burnt, brown and ugly."

"Why are you complaining? We're the ones about dead. Can't you see how withered we are?" screamed the roses.

The shrub, apple tree and oak tree had a complaint too. They all complained and complained.

There were periods of heavy rainfalls throughout the autumn season. When the rains ceased, the plants felt like they just had a refreshing autumn bath that sent tingling sensations all over and down to their roots. And there was a change that took placed among the friends.

"Look," shouted the pine tree. "The oak and apple trees are covered with colorful leaves of yellow, brown, and red. And so is the bushy shrub. Look at me, I have a more vibrant green color than before."

The few remaining roses oohed and aahed with curiosity.

The whole bunch still complained. Each one wanted to be like the other. The bushy shrub had colorful leaves, but he felt he should be as tall as the trees. The roses were upset because they couldn't change colors at all, only to turn brown and then die. The pine tree complained because he had no leaves. The oak tree griped because he couldn't bear any fruit like the apple tree. The apple tree said her branches were always heavy and aching from the loads of apples that she bore. There was no satisfaction among the plants. They stopped talking among themselves. For two whole days they did not mumble a word or even looked at each other.

Just as they least expected two humans approached the forest. They were searching for good trees to use for lumber. The plants had never seen a human before but had heard about them. There was a loud buzzing noise heard in the midst of the forest.

"Oh my gosh. What is going on?" asked the shrub.

The others were slow to answer. The apple tree finally spoke up.

"I think it is some sort of machine. I can see dust flying within the forest." There was a loud noise heard in the forest that sounded similar to a thousand firecrackers popping. That noise was heard again and again.

"Oh no, they are removing trees from the forest. See how they slice them up," screamed the pine tree.

"I wish I could hide," cried the bushy shrub.

"Why should you? These walking creatures just want trees not shrubs," said the last pink rose.

The other roses had already died.

"Well, we are going to have to do something because I don't want to be cut down," shouted the oak tree.

"We? What do you mean we? I barely can protect myself," nervously said the pine tree.

They whispered among themselves and devised a plan. The two humans entered the edge of the forest where the plants were. They headed directly for the oak tree which was about to be cut down.

"Help me," cried the oak tree.

Just as the humans were about to start up the saw, they were suddenly being attacked. The apple tree dropped apples on the human's heads. Acorns spinning like speeding bullets were discharged from the oak tree. When the humans fell down, the pine tree sent cones flying into their faces. One of the humans fell on the prickly sticks of the bushy shrub as he tried to get up. A thorny rose pricked the other human. The humans ran out of the forest as fast as they could. They left behind their machines, hats and other tools.

"Yeah, we showed them," shouted the apple tree.

"We sure did," replied the bushy shrub. "That was teamwork."

At that moment there was silence. They all looked at each other. They smiled and apologized for their ridiculous behavior. Now they understood why God had made each one of them differently. He had a purpose for doing so. It is better to be appreciative of who or what you are rather than complain. They remained friends for many years to come. The machines, hats, and tools are still there as a reminder to the forest friends.

Whipping Conscience

"I've told you several times before Blake that stealing is wrong and it leads to bigger crimes. I wish there were someone that can make you understand. It seems like I can't," cried Ms. Johnson.

Ms. Johnson constantly stayed on Blake's case for stealing. She would always ask Blake does his conscience bother him when he steals? He would always reply no.

"Blake you are 18 years old. You need to find a job or go to school," demanded Ms. Johnson.

One cool October night Blake and two of his friends stole some jewelry from the mall. Luck again was on their side. They did not get caught. They hid out in an old abandon apartment complex on the Lower East Side of Harlem. The idea of stealing never seemed to be a threat to them. They always thought it was an amusing and easy way to gain access to the things they wanted without having to work for it.

"Boy, I like this watch I got. And I sure like that gold necklace you have Blake," said RJ.

"Hey man does your conscience ever bother you? My mother asked me that ALL-THE-TIME. I am so sick of her asking me that same question over and over again. I just tell her no so she can get out of my face."

They looked at each other, shrugged their shoulders and laughed out loud.

"Hell no. I never think about anything like that," said Chris.

About that time somebody knocked at the door.

"Who is that?"

"I don't know. No body knows we are here. So why would somebody be knocking at the door?" asked Blake.

"I don't know, but I'll ask who it is. Who is there?" asked RJ.

Nobody replied. The guys pulled opened the door. They saw no one.

"Somebody is messing with us. It must have been an old drunk wino looking for some dam place to lay down," said Chris.

"Yeah, shut the door."

The guys continued to rant and rave about their stolen merchandise, and then they finally went home.

On his way home, Blake bumped into a dark hooded stranger.

"Hey man, get out of my way. I ain't got any time for no stuff."

About that time the dark hooded stranger grabbed Blake and started shaking him. Blake was pushed around, kicked and even whipped. Blake didn't know what to think. He was too shaken up to fight back. Blake immediately headed for home. He ran all the way.

"Don't ever say your conscience doesn't bother you because it does," yelled the dark hooded stranger.

When Blake arrived home, he was completely out of breath and too scared to even think. He went straight to bed. He did not tell his mother what had happened. Blake still had his stolen piece of jewelry.

The next morning Ms. Johnson had gone to work and Blake was still at home in the bed. He observed the stolen jewelry.

"I guess I'll sell this to make a few dollars," smiling as he nodded his head up and down.

Suddenly, the windows and doors opened up and paper went flying everywhere.

"No you will not," said the voice.

"Who said that?" asked Blake.

It was the dark hooded stranger. It slowly removed the hood. Blake gasped for air and moaned because the face under the hood resembled Blake's face.

"I am your conscience and your worst nightmare," said the dark tall hooded stranger."

Blake yelled and yelled. He covered his eyes so he could not see himself.

"You're going to learn a new lesson in stealing, how not to steal. You told your mother that your conscience doesn't bother you. It should and it will. I am your worse nightmare. Meet your conscience. Every time you steal, you arouse me and cause me to partake in your devious deeds. You are always contemplating if you're going to get caught and go to jail. Well wonder no more. I'm here to stay and to straighten you out."

Conscience gave Blake a good whipping. For days conscience worried Blake so much that Blake could not sleep at night. He tossed and turned. He would not show his face in public. He feared that everyone was watching him. He hurt psychologically and emotionally. Blake could feel this whipping. It drained him of his energy. It made him feel hopeless and useless. It was like conscience physically gave Blake a whipping.

"That will teach you. If you steal again, I'll be back to give you some more. You are never too old to get a whipping as long as I am around."

Blake woke one morning feeling uneasy and paranoid. He shivered at the thought that conscience may be standing over him, but it was his mother. Blake noticed he was lying on the floor, and that's when he extended his arms toward his mother for a hug. He began to cry.

"Boy what is wrong with you? Why are you on the floor?"

"Conscience whipped me," Blake mumbled.

"A girl whipped you?" replied Ms. Johnson.

"No, my conscience. Why didn't you tell me it was real? I thought you were messing with my head when you kept asking me about my conscience."

Ms Johnson shook her head. She was puzzled. She came to the conclusion that a few of the guys had beaten Blake up and he was too ashamed to admit the truth.

"One thing is for sure; I will not steal anymore. I'm going to do the right thing for now on. Where is the newspaper? I need to find a job."

Several weeks later, Blake went back to the mall. He saw his old friends. They were up to some mischief and wanted Blake to join them. Blake thought about it, but changed his mind very quickly. He tried to convince his friends not to steal.

"Okay, go ahead and steal. You will see just like I did."

Blake left his friends and went his separate way. Just as he was leaving the mall, conscience appeared.

"Since you thought about me, I decided to check on you to see how you were doing."

"I am doing fine. I have stopped stealing and decided to find a job."

"That is very good! Now if you will excuse me, I know of two young men that are in desperate need of a conscience whipping."

The Brown Bag

As Claire Carson pulls the van into the supermarket parking lot, inquisitive eight-year-old Claudia zooms in on an old man carrying a brown paper bag into the supermarket. The van couldn't have stopped fast enough for Claudia. She was eager to jump out of the van as it came to a screeching halt.

"Mom, will you please hurry up. I need to see something," demanded Claudia.

Claire looks at Claudia. "Wait, young lady. You don't rush me. Besides why are you in such a big hurry? You see I have to release these seatbelt straps so that your brother can get out. Just hold your horses. Besides what do you see anyway?"

"I saw a man carrying a brown paper bag into the supermarket," replied Claudia.

"So what?"

"He maybe trying to steal something and I'm going to catch him."

"Girl, mind your own business and leave that old man alone. He is a stranger. What have I told you about strangers? Or have you forgotten?"

"No, I have not. Okay mom, I'll be good."

Claudia sighs and stomps her foot. Claire gives Claudia a mean look to let her know she was not playing. The three finally enter the supermarket. Claudia was in search of the old man. The very moment Claire reaches onto the shelf to get a can good, Claudia slyly sneaks away. Claudia is like a cop on a stakeout. Claire sees Claudia, but Claudia doesn't see her. Claire is about to give Claudia a smack on her butt, when Claudia yells out, "Hey mister, I see you. Oh you are NASTY AND DIRTY!"

Not knowing what is going on, the old man turns around in surprise. He looks at the Carson family. He stares at Claire for a second as if he knows her.

"May I help you with something?" he inquired.

"Yeah, I...."

"Settled down child. Mister, my daughter has this crazy notion that she saw you carrying a brown paper bag into this store and thinks that you are about to—I'm too embarrassed to say. Let's see—-steal something?"

"So she does? Well, I'm not. And besides little children like you need to tend to your own business. Now excuse me," griped the old man.

"We are sorry for bothering you," said Claire.

The old man makes his departure down another aisle without looking back. Claire looks at Claudia and does not say a word. Claudia knew what time it was. Claire finished gathering the things she needed for the picnic. She pays for the items and heads straight for the park.

Claudia was on her best behavior because she knew she had a whipping coming.

"Okay children, we are going to have some fun while we are at the park today. One of you needs a good beating because you got out of line. I'm still burning with anger because of the incident earlier, but we will let it slide and hope it does not happen again, right?"

"Yes mam," they both replied.

It was a great day to be at the park. The family was having a wonderful time. Claire wished that her husband Dr. Howard Carson, a cardiologist could join them, but his schedule was too hectic that day for fun in the park. The family played horseshoes, swinging on the swings, jump rope, and anything else that was fun. While they were playing ball, Little Ryan accidentally threw the ball into some high shrubbery. Claudia goes after the ball. As she proceeds to return, her interest takes notice of an object lying on one of the park benches. It appears to be a brown paper bag.

Claudia makes her way toward the brown paper bag. Being nosey and cautious, Claudia picks up the bag and pries inside. She discovers a dingy toothbrush, toothpaste, a wash rag, a bar of soap, deodorant, two pair of socks, a handkerchief, and a Bible full of old loose paper. Claudia recognizes this scenario. The old man was homeless. But where was the old man? She looks around to find him and he was no where in sight.

About that time Claire and Ryan came whizzing around the shrubbery looking for Claudia. Claudia looks at Claire. Claire is so furious that she has to hesitate a moment before she whips Claudia.

"Child, what are you doing? For once, can't you stop being so mischief?"

Claudia did not hear a word her mother had asked her. Instead, she proceeded to talk about what she had just found.

"Mom, do you remember that man with the brown paper bag?"

"Yes," said Claire angrily.

"Well, this belongs to him. Look inside."

"I will not. This does not belong to you. Leave other people things alone. When will you learn to stop meddling?"

Claire takes the brown paper bag into her hand. Slowly she pulls the bag open. She saw all the same contents that Claudia saw. Claire pulls out the Bible and flips through the pages. She found some old letters that were written by children. She saw several pictures, but there was this one picture that held her attention. It was a picture of a woman holding two children. Claire takes a closer look at the picture. The expression on her face indicated to Claudia that something was wrong.

"Oh my God, no it can't be? It just can't be?" sobbed Claire.

"What is it mom?" asked Claudia.

Claire started to explain, but then she paused. She thought it was best to wait before she mentioned anything to Claudia. Claire glimpses at the picture one more time and hurriedly places it back into the Bible; she then puts the brown bag back on the bench. The Carson family returned to their picnic in the park.

Sitting nearby observing intensely was the old man. He had been watching the Carson family from afar. Why didn't he retrieve his brown paper bag, when the Carsons were prying in his business? It was like he wanted them to find that brown paper bag.

The Carsons continued their family fun time together up until the wee hours of the evening. Everybody was worn out and wanting to leave. As they were leaving, Claire noticed an ambulance in the park. She thought to herself, "Somebody has gotten too hot and exerted him or herself." The Carsons loaded up their van and headed for home.

Later that evening while the Carson family was having a wonderful well-prepared dinner; Claudia began to tell her father what had happened that day. Claire filled in all the naughty details about Claudia's behavior at the supermarket. Dr. Carson gave Claudia a good scolding.

"So honey, how was your day at work?" asked Claire.

"Hectic as usual. But there was this one old man that came through the emergency room. Somebody found him at the park. He was having a heart attack. At least that's what it appeared to be. Come to find out his heart is fine. We admitted him for an overnight observation."

Claire is curious. She wonders if that is the same old man with the brown paper bag that they saw in the park? She quickly gets the children off to bed so that she can be alone with her husband.

"Claire, why are you putting the children to be so early?"

"They are tired and exhausted from all that fun at the park today. Besides you and I need to be alone."

"Now that's my girl. You know how to keep your man happy."

Claire looks at Dr. Carson, she rolls her eyes and giggles.

"Get your mind out of the gutter. That's not what I mean."

"Oh well, so much for making daddy happy. What's on your mind sweetheart?"

"That old man you saw in the emergency room, was he carrying a brown paper bag?" asked Claire.

Dr. Carson thinks for moment and answers, "You know I think I did hear one of the ER nurses say he had a brown bag. They said the bag contained some items such as toothpaste, soap, a washrag, and some other items. Oh yeah, there was a Bible that contained a lots of old papers."

Claire drops her head and turns away. Dr. Carson curiously looks at Claire. He inquires what is going on.

"Honey, I may be wrong. That old man may be my long lost father. I found a picture of my family—mother, my sister and me in the early years of my childhood."

"How can you be for sure?" asked Dr. Carson.

"I recognize the picture. We had that picture taken at the county fair. My father wasn't in the picture because he was on the run from the law. It was a mistaken identity. There was a murder in town and it was presumed that my father was the guilty one. My father was out of town at the time. When my father got wind of the news, he stayed away. The real murderer and my father resembled each other—they were twins. My father was shorter. My mother and father kept in touch. That's how he received that picture of us. By the time it was discovered who the real murderer was my father was on his way back home to us. He was tired of being away and playing this 'hideout game'. But he ran into some trouble. I guess there were those who were tired of waiting on him to return so they searched for him. Mother became devastated and went into depression once she found out that father was killed. Mother recovered, but she was never the same again."

Dr. Carson looked at Claire with compassion and dismay. He pulled her close to him and gave her a loving hug. He did not say one word. But he knew what Claire was thinking.

The next morning at the breakfast table, Dr. Carson suggests to Claire not to get her hopes up incase this is not who she thinks it is. Claire understood and nodded yes. As soon as the children finish eating breakfast, Claire drives them to the babysitter.

Claire could feel her adrenaline pulsating as she hurriedly rushes to the St. Memorial Hospital. As she leaves her vehicle, her steps get slower and slower. She is thinking in her mind what if she is wrong and this is not her father? But then on the other hand she will never know until she asks. She takes a deep breath and continues walking toward the patient's room.

Claire quietly knocks at the door, no answer. She knocks again, still no answer. She enters the room. She does not see anyone. She sees the Bible lying on the nightstand. She walks toward the Bible and picks it up. She opens up the Bible to where the picture is located. Claire takes the picture out and gently rubs her fingers over the faces on the picture. She is startled by the sound of a clearing throat. Then a voice saying, "May I help you?"

She immediately closes the Bible and turns around. There they were the two of them facing each other. The old man didn't look so bad now that he had had a clean shave and a bath. As a matter of fact, he looked rather handsome for an old timer.

"Oh no, not you lady. What are you doing in my room? Checking—no let me see your daughter sent you to see if I stole something. You rich people make me sick. Why don't you leave me alone? Wait, this is my opportune time to have you thrown out. Isn't that the way you rich people do it?"

"Sir I am not here to bother you."

"Well, it sure looks that way. If my mind serves me right, I don't remember calling you."

"You are right and you did not. But the other day in the park my daughter found your brown paper bag. She looked inside the bag and so did I."

"Oh, I see, you all are thieves. You prey on poor people like me. Nobody would ever guess that you are thieves because you have that rich look. Besides who would believe me if I tried to convince somebody that you were stealing from me? People would think I am crazy."

"No we weren't trying to steal. We, I mean I found this picture in your Bible. Where did you get this picture?

"That's none of your business. Can't a person carry a picture of someone without a lot of questions being asked? I bet you have pictures in your purse. You don't see me asking what pictures are you carrying in your purse. Now do you?"

Claire goes into her purse and pulls out a picture mounted in a pewter 5" x 7" frame. She removes the picture from the Bible places them side by side for comparison so that the old man could see them. The old man drops his head and snatches the pictures from Claire's hand.

"Tell me, are you who I think you are? Start talking," demanded Claire.

The old man became hesitant for a moment then he proceeded to talk. Claire knew of course, people were scandalous. They would stoop to any means to get on the good side of people they thought were rich. She was hoping this was not the case, but the case of a lost individual trying to get back home.

He started from the beginning. He gave specific, concrete, and explicit details from the time he met Claire's mother, Claire's birth, and up until the time he was suppose to be dead. Everything was as Claire had remembered. But she was still skeptical. Anybody can pretend they are someone else by perpetrating their lifestyle, background, and obtaining other pertain information that would be suitable for the cause. And the picture, let's say you can simply steal it. All these things pondered through Claire's mind as she stared at the old man.

The old man sat at the edge of the bed. He did not make a move, or try to be convincing to Claire. There were only two ways to prove that he may or may not be Claire's father. She asked to see his left foot. If the small toe was missing which resulted from an accident when he was ten years old, was the first proof. He showed Claire the left foot and the small toe was missing. Claire felt a sigh of joy.

Next Claire checked his right arm for a scar that extended from his elbow to his armpit. He received this scar trying to slide into home base while playing baseball at the age of 12. The old man raised his arm and there was the scar. Claire dropped her purse and hugged the old man's neck. "Daddy, it's you. I knew it was you."

The old man's eyes filled with tears as Claire embraced him. They both were crying and sobbing when Dr. Carson entered into the room. First he was in shocked because he was bewildered. Then it dawned on him that Claire had found her father. This was a family reunion moment. The atmosphere was mellow, full of joy, happiness, and praises of thanks.

There was one thing that bothered Claire. Why was her father carrying around a brown paper bag? Where did he live? Where has he been? He explained to her that's what his life had become after all that hiding and running, especially when everybody thought he was dead. The items in the brown paper bag were his only means of hope. The brown paper bag was like a road map directing him back to his family.

"Hmm," she said. "So you did not recognize who I was?" she asked.

"No I did not. Sweetheart you have to understand it has been years since I last saw you, your mother or sister. And you probably wonder why I disappeared for good and suddenly resurface this day and time?"

She looked at him waiting for an answer. He continued to explain.

"I had no way of contacting my family. I did not know who to trust; and plus I had already put my family through enough. So I disappeared. It was only a year ago that I decided to find my family. The only memories I had of my family were this picture I carried in this Bible. I'm not asking for anything. I'm just an old man too tired to run any more. I figured before they come to get me, the right thing to do was at least find my family and to let them know I was alive."

The room was quiet except from the sounds of sobbing tears from Claire. Dr. Carson did not know what to say. He did not know whether to send this old timer on his way because of painful memories he brought back to his wife, or to hug him because he filled a void in his wife's life. Dr. Carson decided to leave it up to Claire. Claire wanted him to stay.

"Okay, let's get well, so you can go to your new home," stated Claire.

The old man, known as Alex Thurston, hugged Dr. Carson and Claire and thanked them for being so understanding. As Claire leaves the room she whispers, "rest well and have a goodnight dad." A cold chill had filled the room as Claire and Dr. Carson departed into the hallway.

Mr. Alex Thurston was dismissed promptly at 8:30a.m. the next morning. Claire was anxious to take him home to meet the children. Well, it was not a welcome homecoming for Alex Thurston by the children. When they saw him sitting on the living room sofa, they ran. Claudia despised him because of the way he talked to her at the supermarket. So she convinced Ryan by saying the old man was mean and nasty.

"Children come here a moment. I want you all…" That's all Claire managed to say before Claudia interrupted her.

"Mom, why is that dirty old man here. I don't like him. Do we have to talk to him?" asked Claudia.

"Claudia, you are being rude. And that was not very nice. I need you to apologize at once."

"Sor-r-r-r-r-r-r-ry."

Claire rolled her eyes at Claudia and pinched her behind the neck.

"You don't have to make her apologize if she doesn't want to. It would not be from her heart. Leave her be. She will come around," said Alex.

Claire explained to the children that the old man was their long lost grandfather. The children did not comment. They just looked nonchalant. Ryan was curious. So he proceeded to talk to Alex. And the conversation was started. Claudia was hesitant, but she finally spoke up.

As the days and weeks passed, Alex enjoyed his new life with his family. He knew he was in heaven. He enjoyed the beautiful home that was surrounded by trees and flowers. His favorite place was the gazebo that rested in the midst of the paradise garden located in back of the house.

"I could easily spend the rest of my life in this garden. It is so breathtaking and full of serenity. This is just the one opportunity for me to enjoy the finer things in life before I leave. I think we should meet here every day for lemonade and cookies. I want to do this before they come to get me," said Alex.

"Grandfather, who is coming to get you, and why do you keep saying that? I don't want you to leave," sobbed Claudia.

"Now don't you cry your eyes out little one. I will be all right. I really don't have a choice in the matter. I'm ready for some delicious cold lemonade that your mother prepares so well."

Claire goes into the house to make the lemonade while the children visit with Alex in the gazebo.

"Claudia talk to me please. I want to hear your sweet voice while I shut my eyes for a moment."

"Okay, grandfather. I'll talk to you. And so will Ryan."

"Alex's eyes were closed the whole time the children were talking to him. When they had finished their version of *Little Red Riding*

Hood, they kissed Alex on both cheeks. He did not respond. Claudia called out to grandfather. He did not answer.

"Ryan I think grandfather is asleep. He can't hear us. Let's see if he wants to lie down," suggested Claudia. "Grandfather would you like to lie down? It would be more comfortable for you if you did."

There was no response. Claudia pinched grandfather on the arm. Still there was no response. She shook Alex as hard as she could, but still no response. Claudia let out a loud shrieking cry, "MOMMY, MOMMY, MOMMY!"

Claire dropped everything and dashed out the door toward the gazebo. By the time she reached the children, she was panting uncontrollably.

"Honey, what is it?"

Claire could see that Claudia's face was wet with tears. Ryan sobbed and whined. Claire looked at Alex. She touched his face. Then she grabbed and pulled his head close to her chest. She continuously rubbed his head over and over again.

"Daddy, why did you leave me? Why? I'm just getting to know you. Daddy please don't leave me."

The children stopped crying. They watched Claire as she cried and sobbed with anger and bitterness. They put their arms around their mother to comfort her.

"Children, your grandfather is gone now. He is gone for good. This is what he meant when he said they were coming to get him. It was God's angels. He is gone to a better place. He died with contentment and a peaceful heart because he found his family with the help of the brown paper bag.

The End

Spirits/Supernatural

The Paintbrush

*H*e is recognized and is considered as one of the world's renowned talented artist. He is known all over the world for his extraordinary oil and water paintings. He has established a reputation that classifies him with some of the greatest artist ever known from the past to the present. It's unsure when his talents began, but by some strange coincident his talents soared exceedingly the very moment he received a golden handle paintbrush from his aunt. This famous artist is known as Peter Vonzeber from Paris France.

Even though Peter's art credibility is known all over the world, he has never had the opportunity to set foot on the soils of the United States. Fortunately by fate the opportunity presented itself for Peter to visit the States. He had the privilege of receiving an invitation to do an art show at the Annual World of Humanities in Arts Award Ceremony. Astonished and surprised, Peter wholeheartedly accepted the invitation to visit the United States.

When the plane landed at the Kennedy Airport, Peter was not expecting to see a crowd waiting to greet him. Peter froze in his tracks when the plane door opened up. The crowd welcomed him with open arms as they screamed, cheered, adorned him with roses, hugs, and handshakes. As the flashing lights begin, anxious reporters, camera crew and the media became overwhelming! And Peter felt honored. A young attractive bachelor like Peter was used to crowds of screaming female admirers, but not like the American women. Also the fact that he is wealthy is another justification for his popularity. He gave them a friendly wave as he walked by the crowd. The Mayor, the Chief of Police of New York, other police officers, and the city's welcoming committee politely escorted him to his limousine.

"The Americans really know how to greet people. They just love to reach out and touch you," exclaimed Peter.

The limousine driver just laughed as he drove away. He hurriedly drove Peter to his hotel to escape the oncoming stampeding crowd.

The hotel attendants treated Peter with the up most kindness. Peter Vonzeber did not have to want for anything. His only concern was the crew and other news media that were waiting to meet him. The hospitality of the crowd was the busboys working the hotel, or maybe they were women pretending to be busboys? Inconveniently, other quests' luggage ended up in his room on several occasions.

Later that night while Peter is sleeping soundly; he is awakened by a very unusual tapping noise coming from his closet. The noise was so faint; Peter felt there was no important need to investigate the noise. He rolled over saying, "What is that noise? I hope it stops."

The rising of the morning dawn set a pattern of exhilaration and cheerfulness as Peter rose to meet the world. He was feeling excited because this was his first visit in the United States. He smiled as he peered out the window to catch a glimpse of the golden sun rising over the city.

His show was set for that evening at the Quartz Lamar Building at four o'clock. Instead of touring the city, he decided he would sit in his room and relax. There was a knock at the door. It was room service. He was served a delicious feast for breakfast. Peter was famished and he devoured every morsel of food.

After breakfast, Peter decided to take inventory of some new paints he had purchased. From his luggage he removed a special brown case that was trimmed in gold. In that case was his wonderful golden handle paintbrush that he valued so highly. He admiringly stroked the handle of the paintbrush. Then he kissed it.

Just as Peter was about to dip the paintbrush into the paint, the brush stung his hand. Peter immediately dropped the paintbrush.

"My word, what's wrong with this brush? That has never happened before."

"Surprise!" shouted the paintbrush. Peter jumped back in astonishment.

"You can talk! You can actually talk. Wait a minute, brushes can't talk."

"I can."

The brush hopped from side to side. Peter, bewildered by the actions of the paintbrush, watched stunningly as it hopped. Peter did not know what to say. He just shook his head and rubbed his eyes several times hoping his mind was not playing tricks on him.

"I am going to pretend I did not see this and begin my painting."

"I don't think so buddy," replied the paintbrush.

"Why do you say that?"

"Because for one reason I am tired of the same old paintings that you do. I want to do something different like abstract painting."

"You know I don't paint like that. That's not my style of painting."

"Well, you better start. Or you'll be sorry."

"Sorry, sorry like how?"

"Fool, who do you think did the painting? Not you of course," laughs the paintbrush. "It was I. You cannot paint a stroke without me. Your painting talents are a joke. You can't even paint a straight line."

"You are crazy, and I am not having this conversation with a paintbrush."

"Okay, go ahead and pick up another brush and try to paint."

Peter did just that. He couldn't. It was like he had forgotten how to paint.

"This is not happening to me," screamed Peter.

He used paintbrush after paintbrush and unsuccessfully was not able to make any kind of artistic stroke.

"Now do you believe me?" asked the paintbrush.

"Not really, but I guess I have to," screamed Peter as he walked toward his bed. He sat down on the bedside with his head hung down. The paintbrush leaped onto his lap and crossed his bristles like a man crosses his legs.

"Okay Peter what's it going to be? My way or no way?" boasted the paintbrush.

Peter grabbed the brush and squeezed it.

"I will not be ruled by a stupid paintbrush."

"Okay, have it your way."

About that time there was a knock at the door, Peter threw the paintbrush on the floor. He answered the door. They were members of the welcoming committee inquiring to see if Peter needed anything before the four o'clock art show. Peter replied that he had everything he needed and he appreciated their generosity and concern.

As soon as the door closed, the paintbrush went on a wild pulsating painting escapade. It painted the walls, bed, and everything else in sight. Peter felt like a maniac strapped in a straightjacket. He tried to stop the paintbrush, but could not do a thing.

"Stop you crazy brush. Stop it right now," demanded Peter.

It would not stop. It continued to paint until all the paint was used up. When the spasmodic paintbrush finally did stop, it painted the final stroke as a mustache across Peter's face.

"Wow, that was fun. I'll take a break for now and do this again later. Oh, by the way you are out of paint," said the paintbrush.

"Good, maybe you will sit still for awhile," grumbled Peter.

"It was one o'clock, Peter needed rest, he was out of paint, and most of all the hotel suite was in a mess. He could not believe all of his paints were used up in a matter of minutes. He called his assistant and requested that he purchase some more paint and supplies.

When the assistant returned, Peter would not let him enter the suite. He did not want the assistant to see the overwhelming mess that had just taken place.

Outraged and pointing his finger at the paintbrush, Peter utters angrily saying, "Now paintbrush, I need you to stop giving me trouble. This hotel suite is in a mess. Look at this room." In a mad fit, Peter slaps the palms of his hands upside his forehead.

"What will the Americans think when they see this hotel room?"

"Hmm, they will think French people have no decency or respect for their property. I don't know, don't care, and who gives a flip? I just want to paint, but in a whole new style. Yuck, your style stinks."

Chasing the paintbrush around the suite and shouting, "I have had enough of you paintbrush, do you hear me?" Suddenly Peter stopped. He looked at the time; it was now three o'clock. It was one hour before the show would start. Peter decided he would give in to the paintbrush until the art show was over.

"Okay paintbrush you win. I will paint the way you desire." As Peter turns and walks away he mumbles, "Then I will fix you later."

Peter Vonzeber left the hotel suite in a complete mess. In hopes of going straight to the airport as soon as the art show is over, Peter prays the mess is not discovered until he is long gone on his flight.

It was four o'clock and the extravagant art show was about to take place downtown at the magnificent Quartz Lamar Building. As the guest gathered in the large distinctive elegant ballroom, Peter patiently waited in a private room. He was about to make his very first public appearance as an artist before the American people. And he wanted to be perfect with no troubles or surprises. Luckily for Peter he had locked up the golden handle paintbrush in the hotel suite. At least that's what he thought.

Peter had now entered the room preparing to make a presentation of one of his artworks. Suddenly, there was a sharp pain piercing him in the chin of his right leg. Peter looks down. It is the paintbrush. Peter panics and gasps for air; then there is a lost for words.

One of the coordinators of the art show asked, "Mr. Vonzeber, are you feeling alright?"

"Ye, ye, ye, yes, I am fine," nervously replied Peter.

Peter looked down again in search of the paintbrush. It was not there. He felt awkward. He tries to look calm, but he can't. He finally spots the paintbrush sitting under a table waving at him. Peter unknowingly jumps with fright.

"Mr. Vonzeber are you sure you are alright?"

"Oh yes, oh yes, just nervous because of my first time in the United States."

As Peter proceeded with the art show, the paintbrush slowly eased its way toward Peter. It was walking and hopping. It was rolling, rolling, and rolling until it reached Peter's feet. Peter tries to elaborate on the paintings as swiftly as he can. When he finishes, he cunningly sneaks over to the paintbrush without making a scene to step on it. The tip of the paintbrush breaks as Peter steps onto the handle. Peter did not move from that spot and no one noticed anything-unusual going on. Everybody was too busy mingling and admiring the paintings.

The paintbrush went mad the very moment that Peter moved his foot. The paintbrush found some paint, jumped into Peter's hand, and had a horrendous field day. It painted everything in its path. The crowd went mad! There was so much commotion of pushing, running over one another, screaming, and falling onto the floor. Peter was painting abstract art.

Peter could not let go of the paintbrush. He tried everything. The paintbrush was confined to his hand; it was clinging like glue. Peter swings his hands in the air, beat it on the tables, and even bit the brush, but the paintbrush was determined to stay put.

The unbelievable scenes that were taking place made Peter feel embarrassed and humiliated. The paintbrush found this to be comical and amusing. Perplexed and bewildered, the crowd stares at Peter. The American people thought he had gone mad.

"It's the paintbrush. It's trying to ruin me. See for yourselves."

Peter extends the paintbrush toward the crowd of people standing nearby. The paintbrush was stiff and motionless. Instantly, it leaps out of Peter's hand onto the head of a lady standing near Peter.

"SURPRISE," shouted the paintbrush.

The lady fainted. The crowd became disturbed and ran with panic. Determined to leave that scene, the crowd pushed their way out the door. Peter tried to run also.

"Where do you think you are going? You and I are partners forever. We are going to paint the town," exclaimed the paintbrush.

"That's what he thinks," Peter said to himself.

While the paintbrush was busy laughing, Peter picks up a lit candle and says, "Paintbrush in celebration of our joint venture, I thinks this calls for a toast."

"Yeah, I think so too."

Peter ignites the bristles of the paintbrush with the burning candle. The paintbrush starts to smoke then it catches on fire. The fire burns rapidly and Peter drops the paintbrush onto the floor. The paintbrush hollers and yells for help until it yells no more. The paintbrush burns completely to ashes. That was the end of the golden handle paintbrush. As for Peter Vonzeber, he caught the first flight out of New York back to Paris France because he was still thinking about that hotel suite. He never set foot on the soil of the United States again.

A Childhood Memory

Now when I think about it, it seems if though the old house was leaning to one side. I believe the floors weren't level especially in the living room. That old house had only four rooms. We had been living in that house since 1963, the year I was born. We lived in that house until I was five years old. Here I am 37 years old thinking and constantly dreaming about that old house. I live in a completely different city than the one where the house is located. So it's not like I pass this house on my every day journey going to and from my points of destination, but I still think of this house. Why?

Maybe there was a bad childhood memory that lingers and clings tightly to my brain cells that won't ever let go. Or maybe just the opposite exits good memories I can't forget. I don't know what the significant reason is, but I know I can't forget about that old house.

This was our Little House on the Prairie. There was no bathroom or running water. There was a long kitchen divided by what suppose to be a bar, one huge bedroom, a living room and then this small mysterious room next to the kitchen

I played alone. We didn't have neighbors that were close enough for me to run next door to play with. My sister, of course, was always somewhere clinging to my mother. So, therefore, I spent a lot of time playing by myself in this mysterious room.

Sometimes if we had company, that stayed overnight, they would sleep in that room. If my memory serves me correctly, I don't remember seeing a bed in that room. Maybe there was one? I do know for sure my grandmother Katie slept in that room, and I know definitely she did not sleep on the floor.

That house always had a cold unfriendly feeling. It seemed if though we were always making fires in a wood-burning stove. I hated that stove. It appeared to be tall and monstrous. The front door of the wood-burning stove resembled a face. And I perceived that face as mean, evil, and full of hatred. The hotter the stove became, the meaner the stove appeared. One could see the red fiery flaming inferno sides that were about to combust at any given moment. The pipe that extended from the stove to the chimney was as red as the coals on the inside of the wood stove. I was terrified to go near that wood stove. Hell was surely inside that wood-burning stove. And I wanted no part of that wickedness.

I will never forget what my father attempted to do to me one day. He tried to lift me on top the wood-burning stove so that I could be standing on it. I screamed and hollered to the top of my lungs. My father was laughing. He apparently found this to be amusing, but I found no humor in his ridiculous games. My father used to drink. So I'm wondering if the alcohol had gotten the best of him? Whether alcohol was or was not involved, I still did not find this amusing.

I will never forget the night I saw that striped black and white snake with pink sponge rollers in its head. Yeah, you heard it right, a snake with rollers in its head. Let me tell you it was no dream. This was for real! I was wide-awake. As a matter of fact, I knew exactly what time of day it was. No I could not tell time, but I could tell the difference between day and night. It was late in the evening.

Well, anyway, I was playing in that mysterious room next to the kitchen. I was playing with my black baldheaded naked doll. My mother, grandmother, and sister were up front in the living room. I decided I would go to the living room to be with the rest of the family.

To my wondering eyes what did I see when I stepped out of the room? Something bizarre, scary, and interesting all at the same time disturbed my train of thought. My mouth flew wide open, and I became petrified. A striped black and white snake with pink spongy rollers in its head looked at me. Can't you imagine what a kid like me must have been thinking when I saw that hideous creature?

The snake hissed to me in a slurring sly sound kind of way. It was trying to communicate to me and I could not understand. I did not want to communicate especially after I saw that old devil work that evil tongue. I remember it standing tall peeping around the side of the kitchen stove glaring at me. I don't see how Eve brought herself to communicate to that serpent in the Garden of Eden. I got plenty of sense. I decided it was time to run and not make any conversation with a snake. I screamed and hollered as loud as I could. I started to cry frantically. My mother and grandmother came as quickly as they could. The snake very quietly disappeared after I started to scream.

"Child what is wrong with you?" asked my mama

I proceeded to tell her after I had caught my breath. She and my grandmother went straight to the kitchen to search for the snake. They searched the whole area and found nothing. I felt so ashamed, but scared.

"I don't see anything. I told you about being so bad and hardheaded. That was the devil coming after you," replied mama.

When they exited the kitchen, I exited with them. My grandmother grabbed me by my hand to comfort me. One thing I did learn and that is to be good and stay out of those back rooms next to the kitchen.

The Straw Hat

*H*ave you ever THOUGHT that you saw something and you really didn't see it? But then you realize that you really did see it? That is what happened to me one hot summer day.

It was weltering hot outside. We (my sister, mother, and I) were watching the 1:30 soap opera on TV. We were visited by our neighbor, my big momma who lived about two minutes away. Whenever big momma goes outside, she always wore a brown straw hat. She never leaves home without it. This is her summer fashion statement.

I was sitting on the green living room sofa that was facing the window. I could see everything that passed by the window. And next to that window sat my sister in a large recliner facing me.

I saw big momma walk pass the window with the big straw hat so I was expecting her to knock on the front door at any time. Several minutes passed and we waited for that little soft knock that she does before she enters our house. No knock. So we waited and waited. I said to my sister, "Big momma is outside horse playing. She is probably waiting to scare us the minute we open that door."

My sister and I went to the door and shouted, "ah ha we gotcha." But we were the ones that were surprised. No one was standing outside the door.

"Now, I know I saw big momma pass that window," I told my sister. It was not my imagination. It was real!"

Later that evening my sister and I paid my big momma a visit. We inquired to her about the afternoon visit at our house. She stated that she has been at home all day. As a matter of fact she never came out of the house until now. I looked at big momma hoping she was not pulling my leg. I saw that she was sincere and telling the truth. I glimpsed at my big momma's hat and noticed it was brown with a strawberry band around it. This hat I saw was white.

"Big momma do you have a new straw hat like maybe a white one?" I asked.

"Child no, I love this old worn out hat that I wear. And I wouldn't dare buy a white straw hat. Do you know how much trouble it is trying to keep those white hats clean?"

That confirmed my suspicion. From then on I learned that when I see a straw hat pass by the window, be aware and be cautious, because that very well may not be big momma.

Someone Called

I used to love to hear stories told by the old folks when I was growing up. My father hunted for a sport. He had hunting buddies that visited us all the time. They would always have some good stories to tell. The stories were so good; they had my full-undivided attention. Sometimes I would forget about the program that I was watching so I could listen to those old hunting tales.

My grandmother told bone-chilling, haunting tales of ghosts, the walking dead, and old wives tales. These stories made my skin crawl. These stories were almost believable! I never saw the walking dead or ghost, but I heard them moving around and whispering names.

When I was eight years old, we lived in a small house on a hill in the country. I will never forget the time I was alone in the living room. I was watching television. I heard someone call my name. I thought it was my mother.

"Tammy, Tammy," it kept saying.

When I answered back, I never heard it again. I thought it was my mother calling me for something.

My mother entered the living room from the kitchen. I asked her did she call me.

"No," she replied.

"Well somebody called me. I thought it was you. I just heard them from that direction calling my name."

She may not have called me, but I did hear that voice. It was as plain as the nose on my face. That's scary to hear someone calling your name, and you never see a face, body, or person to go with that voice.

I have often heard the old folks say that we shall hear and see things of the unnatural pertaining to this world.

Four O'clock

Tick, tock, tick, tock was the sound of that old clock beside my bed. It was 10:00p.m. and I was not sleepy. I guess I will stay up late again tonight watching old movies. This was something I thought I never would be doing for seven months. I was terminated from my job and could not find a decent job for months. Oh, I tried applying for everything possible when I finally got fed up looking for work in my field.

In the meantime when I was not looking for work, I would be at home enjoying myself. Lots of times I became depressed when I could not find work, but I tried to make the best of it.

It was early autumn and the weather felt wonderful! Every morning I would get up between the hours of eight and nine o'clock; I would clean the house then sit down to watch my favorite soaps until late afternoon. For a moment, I thought I was on a vacation. Then sometimes I felt totally bored. Whenever I really wanted to express myself, I would write poetry or a story. I especially loved writing poems. I would sit on the back porch and gaze into the thick woods that were in back of our house. I listened to the chirping of all the birds as they cascaded throughout the trees. Just sitting and listening to nature from my back porch was mellow to me. It was so peaceful! Sometimes I would sit in the same old spot until dusk dark. My old gray cat named Asriel always kept me company whenever I sat on the porch. This was not the best of fun, but I had to do something to keep my mind busy and not think of unemployment.

Every now and then I would sneak off into the woods in back of our house. I could see where farmers had cut trees and bushes to make lumber. Then I would escape to this big old field that was covered extremely with tall brown grass. The grass of the field resembled a grassy savanna of Africa. I spotted a herd of deer that were playing and jumping like kids. They never noticed me. I have never seen so many deer at one time! Exploring that area seems exciting to me. I had nobody to answer to and nobody to bother me. I still thought about work. I thought about the things I could be buying or shopping for.

My mother was at home with me, but to tell the truth, she was not much company. She hardly ever talked to me. Lots of times I would just strike up a conversation or just ask her a question just for the sake of it. We never made that transition to have a normal conversation between the two of us.

It was getting late in the evening so I commenced to move into the house. I would do my same old night routine. I would take my bath and put on my nightclothes, and then I would get ready for my nighttime shows. Ten o'clock would roll around so fast and I would not be sleepy. I would find old movies on TV and would watch them way up into the wee hours of the morning.

One night when we were all in bed, I heard this loud noise. I t was four o'clock in the morning. There was this thumpty bump noise and moving of objects like someone was throwing things around in the bathroom closet. It became louder and louder. At one point, I thought it was my mother looking for something, but not at four o'clock in the morning. You could hear things falling, breaking, and crashing. I was puzzled but too terrified to move. I desperately wanted to get up and see what that noise was, but my legs would not move. That noise lasted for quite some time. Finally, I fell asleep.

When I woke up, it was daylight. I hurried to my sister's room to ask her did she hear the noises in the bathroom closet earlier this morning. She replied that she did. She could not identify the noise. I asked my mother was she up at four o'clock in the morning looking for something in the bathroom closet. She replied no, but needless to say she also heard the noise. So we all proceeded to the bathroom closet. We opened the closet door and to find to our surprise nothing was ever moved. Everything was still in place. We expected the closet to be a total disaster from the way the noises sounded. We were perplexed and puzzled so we closed that closet door immediately. I stated jokingly that that was a spirit or ghost. My sister nodded her head in agreement.

It was another typical day for me. I had been job-hunting, but nothing definite. Since it was so hot and muggy, we all sat around watching television. I thought about what had happened earlier that morning. I hope it does not happen again tonight.

Finally, night came and I was standing outside on the porch listening to the croaking of the tree frogs and crickets. I watched as the fireflies fluttered and flickered with gleams of light in the night sky. Nature own plants released wild aromatic fragrance that caused the nerve endings to be aroused in my nose. These fragrances traveled through the brisk air.

A whippoorwill was outside my window singing with the other night creatures. I fell asleep listening to that whippoorwill. When I woke up, I heard a dog barking foolishly. His barking irritated me and reminded me of my being unemployed. Normally, I watched TV when I woke up, but this time I just grabbed a snack and went back to bed.

Thumpty, bump, bang I leap straight up in the bed. There's that noise again. I looked at the clock. It was four o'clock exactly the same time the noise occurred the morning before. I sat up in bed for a moment to listen.

"What is that noise?" I asked myself. "Maybe it was a large rat? But a rat could not make that much noise, can it? Maybe it's that walking spirit?"

The noise sounded like demolition work. I grew curious, but not enough to the point where I wanted to get up and investigate that noise. I waited to see how long that noise would last. It continued for one whole hour. Then it stopped. I never heard that noise any more that morning.

The next morning my sister hurried to my bedroom. She said she heard the noise again herself. I said it lasted for one hour. Once again, we proceeded to the bathroom to investigate the matter. Everything was still in placed. Nothing was moved. My mother mentioned that might have been our father returning to search for something. I responded to my mother, "That was not funny. I did not want to believe it, but I have heard of this. If it was father, I hope he finds what he needs. He scares me with all that bumping and knocking that he makes in the closet."

I was feeling extremely elated because of a job interview that I had scheduled for Thursday morning at 9:30. This job was with a newspaper company for an assistant editor. I was running late. I became frustrated at myself. I had to rush to get dressed and I hated to get dressed in a hurry. I was determined to look my best for this interview.

I noticed my clock was not running. It had stopped. Maybe I forgot to wind it up? But I did wind up my clock before I went to bed, but it's strange that it stopped at four o'clock.

While on my way to the interview, it occurred to me that the clock stopped exactly at the same time that the noise started. I decelerated the speed of the car. I could feel myself getting nervous. My palms were sweaty. What does this mean or does this mean anything? I psyched myself into believing it was just pure coincidental that the clock stopped at four o'clock. That noise did not have anything to do with that clock stopping at four o'clock. I came to my senses and concentrated totally on the interview.

I was a nervous wreck by the time I arrived at the Newspaper Company. Trying to hold my composure was not easy. I tried reading a magazine, doing a crossword puzzle, and even filing my nails. Mr. Carter finally called me into his office. He looked very distinguished and well dressed. He wore a dark blue tailored suit with matching necktie and socks. Those dreamy eyes of his stared at me the moment after I seated myself. He could see straight through me. He could tell I was nervous.

We heard a loud thumpty bump noise down the hall. It was almost similar to the noises I had heard in my bathroom closet. I could feel my eyes enlarging and my left leg began to twitch. "That noise is following me! It's an omen," I said to myself.

Mr. Carter stopped his interview with me to excuse himself so he could investigate the noise down the hall. When he returned, he had this peculiar look on his face. I asked him was everything okay.

"I don't know," he said. "The construction crew was suppose to be working on the rooms down the hall, but apparently they are not working. Nobody is there. I guess they had the day off. Everything is still in place just as they left it."

I got really scared after he told me that. Mr. Carter ended his interview with me in 20 minutes. The interview went well and I was pleased. He said he would give me a call before five o'clock that evening if I got the job. All the way home I pondered about the noise I had heard at my interview. It was so unusual to hear the same noise but in a different place. As soon as I got home, I raced to tell my mother and sister what had happened at the interview. They just shook their heads and both replied, "Sure is strange."

The afternoon was cloudy and hot, but a cool breeze would blow every now and then to cool things off. I relaxed by reclining on the back porch listening and watching the birds in the trees. Being so peaceful and quiet I dozed off to sleep.

My sleep was disturbed. My sister woke me to say that I had a phone call. It was Mr. Carter from the Newspaper Company telling me I got the job. As soon as I hung up the phone, I leaped for joy and ran outside shouting, "I got the job, I got the job."

I went back into the house to check the time. I had slept for a pretty good while. I looked at my clock; it had four o'clock. Well of course my clock would be wrong because it had stopped running earlier this morning. Then I checked the other clocks in the house. They had the same time—four o'clock. A cold chill ran over my complete body. I did not know the reason being but four o'clock seems to be a destined time for me. The noise, the clock stopping, and Mr. Carter calling me about the job were all coincidental events occurring at the hour of four o'clock. I tried to convince myself these events do not mean any thing and neither are they related to any cause.

The gray sky became darker as the thunderstorm moved in. It was so dark it seemed like nighttime. I lay across my bed and dozed off while looking out the window. When I woke up it was 10:00p.m. and pitch black. The storm must have knocked out the electricity.

I felt my way around the room to slide on my pajamas so that I could go to bed. I tossed and turned for a long time and when I woke up it was four o'clock. "Not again," I said to myself.

This time I did not hear any noises. I checked my clock to make sure it was right and running. A hot breeze flew cross my back. I lay motionless for a moment then I relaxed. Tonight I will get some rest because there is a storm and that's the only noise I'm intending to hear. GOOD NIGHT!

A Fearful Night's Journey

The Origin of Departure

All I wanted to do was go home, shower and go to bed. And that's exactly what I did. I remember falling into a calm tranquilize state of relaxation as the thunderstorm soothed me into a peaceful sleep.

The violent turbulence and raging of the intense storm showed no mercy for mankind, as swift winds and heavy rains thrashed down on mother earth. The explosive sounds of thunder rumbled and vibrated throughout the lands as the electrifying flashes of lighting lit the madden skies. The atmosphere indicated a terrible storm stirring outside.

One can only experience great pain piercing the heart after looking upon the faces of the bitter and homely children of the orphanage. These pitiful souls displayed feelings of hopelessness and low spirits as they wait for the opportune time to be adopted. St. Peter's Orphanage was the oldest orphanage in the country of Britain.

They were just finishing dinner and preparing for Christian emphasis before bedtime, when an immense streak of lightening flashed in the sky followed by a great crashing that was heard in front of the building. Blasting like dynamite, the lightening rolled like a loud whip that stretched for miles, as the magnitude of thunderous echoes deafened one's ears.

The screaming of the frightful children drowned the roar of thunder.

"Ms. Corlett, you need to check on the children in the west wing. Then check the east wing also," demanded Mr. Farley.

"Ye-e-es sir. I will get right on it sir," nervously she replied.

As she proceeded to check on the children, the lights went out. Screams again were heard all over St. Peter's Orphanage. "Quickly," someone shouted, "find some candles and lamps. We must have some lights immediately."

The whole staff at the orphanage hurriedly searched for lamps and candles.

"Oh yes, look what I have found. I found the candles!" shouted Ms. Royal. "This candle is for me, you all can light your own."

Within in minutes light could be seen in the main dining room of the orphanage. The screaming and shouting ceased. But the rain did not. It only rained harder. The headmaster decided that everyone should move to the chapel. As soon as they gathered together the headmaster called for prayer. Everyone joined hands and prayed.

The children felt much safer. Some of the children fell asleep, while others try to brave the storm by watching and listening to every unpredictable move made by the storm.

Two hours had passed and finally one of the staff members Ms. Ace spoke up. "I think the children need to return to their rooms. They seemed to be more relaxed now."

"No, we shall all stay here together for the night," responded Mr. Farley.

"I think it's silly to continue to stay here for the night when they have warm beds that they could be sleeping in," said Ms. Ace.

"I don't think you quite understand. It's not the warmth I'm concerned about. It is their safety," said Mr. Farley.

"Sh-sh-sh-sh-sh you two. Stop that nonsense. You both are disturbing the children. Take your arguments outside and leave the children alone," demanded Ms. Corlett.

The two suddenly became quiet and walked away in separate directions. An unexpected exploding sound of thunderclap caused the already apprehensive and disturbed children to rage in fear as they bundled more closely for comfort. Mr. Farley looked out the window and saw a bolt of lightening strike a large oak tree near the orphanage. The tree caught on fire and fell on the building. The building began to burn.

Another ball of lightening struck the orphanage and split the walls on the east wing of the building. Mr. Farley was doing his best to calm the children, but it did no good. Instead, he left the chapel in search of damages caused by the lightening. He had checked every wing except the east wing, which is the lowest part of the building near a hill.

As Mr. Farley approached the door to the east wing, he heard a swift rapid moving noise. He swallowed hard hoping in his mind; the noise was not what he was thinking. He quickly reached for the doorknob, but let go just as quick. Reluctant and hesitant of what might exist behind the closed door, he leaned his head against the door looking downward and saying, "oh Father, please have mercy upon us." His eyes were fixed upon the stream of water that was pushing its way under the door.

When he did open the door, he was hit in the face. He could see a huge hole extending from the ceiling down the wall, and onto the floor. Damages caused by the lightening had the building burning from the fallen oak tree. And the feeling of cold water rushing at his body caused the great forces of the water to sweep Mr. Farley off his feet and sent him sailing down the hall corridors of the orphanage. He managed to grasp hold of the side of a wall. Panting and puffing, he forcefully tried to warn the others of the event that just happened.

Ms. Corlett steps into the hall and sees Mr. Farley lying in the rushing waters on the floor. "Oh my God, Mr. Farley are you alright? Can you hear me?" He manages to wave at her. He crawls to his knees and tells Ms. Corlett to get everyone to dryer shelter for safety.

Immediately, Ms. Corlett goes back to the chapel. She warns everyone that they are in danger and need to seek shelter for safety.

The water unmercifully continued to pour in at an accelerated speed. By now all the halls were flooded, and water was ankle deep. The building continued to burn on the east end. As the last of the staff members exited the chapel, Mr. Farley was making his way toward the chapel. Two staff members assisted Mr. Farley to safety.

"Where are we seeking shelter?" asked Mr. Farley.

"We are going to the attic," replied one of the staff members.

"Oh, Mr. Farley, thank heavens you made it. I was worried about you," cried Ms. Corlett.

"You know nothing can happen to an old goat like me. Remember I'm invincible," smiles Mr. Farley.

One by one children and staff members hurried to safety. The water was rising rapidly. Excitement, fear, and chaos caused the children to start pushing, shoving and acting disorderly. Some children and staff members fell back into the cold and unfriendly rushing waters as they tried to elevate themselves into the attic. They yelled and shouted for help as they struggled to escape the rapid currents of the rushing waters. Safely everyone made it into the attic.

"How long will we have to stay here?" asked Ms. Ace.

"Nobody knows for sure. At least until the rain has stopped," replied Mr. Farley.

Feeling frigid and timid the children tried to establish themselves as comfortable as they could in the attic. That was hard considering the overwhelming ordeal they just experienced. Mr. Farley and Ms. Corlett together had personally tried to comfort each of the children. Other staff members tried to help out, but they weren't as effective as Mr. Farley and Ms. Corlett. Within an hour's time, all the children were calm and lying down peacefully. What would happen from this point on depended on the storm?

Two hours had passed and the early morning was approaching. The raging storm had ceased. What had sounded like drums banging on a sidewalk now sounded like the tapping of a cat's walk. Peace was now in the air.

The silence was broken by the whisper of a child saying, "We're moving." A little boy subconsciously woke up to say he felt like they were moving. Of course, no one paid him any attention because they thought he was talking in his sleep.

Mr. Farley jumped up and staggered toward the attic window so he could look out. In view of his eyesight, his optic vision surveyed the dim surroundings. He shouted, "I can't see a thing. But I do hear lots of water splashing. Are there any more candles available? Perhaps someone could search for a kerosene lamp as well?" They started the search for a kerosene lamp.

"Look, what I have found," screamed Ms. Royal. "A kerosene lamp. As a matter of fact, here is another one. We have two kerosene lamps." Everyone cheered.

A male staff member lit one of the kerosene lamps and handed it to Mr. Farley and Mr. Farley held it out the window. "Blessed be the name of Jesus Christ," exclaimed Mr. Farley.

"What is it?" inquired Ms. Ace.

Mr. Farley was silent. He slid to the floor and dropped the lamp. The others could tell by Mr. Farley's actions that it was evident that they were surrounded by water. Ms. Royal snatched the lamp from Mr. Farley. She was determined to see what was going on. She awkwardly waved the lamp out the window and shrieked. The kerosene lamp fell from Ms. Royal's hand and into the water. The children begin to whine and cry.

"We have only one lamp left and it's our only means of light to see by while we are confined in this attic. We do not need to check the conditions outside because the sun will be rising soon," said Mr. Farley. "In the meantime we have to be patient and wait this thing out."

Time passed slowly. What seemed like a couple of hours-felt more like a lifetime. Daytime was approaching. A glitch of the early dawn could be seen creeping through the attic window as everyone rose one by one. Ms. Royal was already standing at the window shaking her head. "We are doomed, just doomed. Look outside. All you can see is miles and miles of water," complained Ms. Royal.

"It can't be true," shouted Ms. Ace. "I just will not believe it."

"Well, look for yourself and tell me what do you think," replied Ms. Royal.

Ms. Ace looked out the window and started to cry. "You might as well get a grip honey. Aint' nobody rescuing us and we ain't going anywhere for a long time," said Ms. Royal. Mr. Farley started comforting Ms. Ace. "Ms. Royal, you are so cruel. How can you say such a thing? You have a wicked heart."

"My heart is not wicked or evil. I just told the truth of what I saw. What would you have told her?"

"The same perhaps. I don't know. Maybe you are right, but I'm not giving up faith."

For an inkling of a second, the building seemed to rock and sway as if it were sailing. The children immediately ran to the window to investigate. They were drifting and wandering on a body of water to where? Nobody knows. The water continued to rise even though the rains had ceased. By now the water had risen to the ledge of the attic window. Everybody was in prayer for a great miracle to happen soon.

Three days had passed. The water, storm, and rain were all in control. Man was now at the mercy of God and nature. At this moment all hope was gone. Misery and despair began to exist. As water oozed through any available cracks and corners, the attic floor became a dry thirsty sponge absorbing all moisture and dampness from the seeping water. Not one dry spot could be found in the attic.

To be surrounded, to lie down, to cry tears of wetness, then to drown and to die, was a horrendous and horrid slow death for these people. This is not fair. Life is not fair. But why, why these people, especially the children? They are innocent individuals. They were seeking a refuge, a salvation, and a hope to live as other normal boys and girls.

They were deprived of the opportunity to have a backyard, a bicycle, a pet, or their own place called home.

These individuals, these soon to be souls will not have to wonder or mourn or cry for help anymore. Their salty tears will be composed as equal elements of this earth that were created by God the father himself. And because of God's compassion, they shall dwell for all eternity into his everlasting home of life. And the waters will wash away all the traces of their organic matter to be free to migrate as the creatures of the air, land and sea. Just as a lid is about to close tightly on a box, a speck of light that waved across the darkened waters spotlighted the almost submerged orphanage. At last hope has come!

I could hear their wretched cries of woes. I could feel their pains of distress and grief. And I could see the tears of sorrow. I woke up to find my pillow saturated from my weeping and mourning throughout the night.

I remained still for the moment to listen for the sound of the raging storm that hypnotized me to sleep. The storm was gone! I crawled to the window to see if nature had left behind any damages. I discovered nature was good to me once more. My world was as beautiful now as it was before I fell asleep. And I was relieved!

The Interstate

It was hard to fall back to sleep after being in that dreadful storm in the middle of nowhere and to witness the almost deaths of those people. But somehow, I managed to feel my eyelids getting very heavy; and I could no longer keep them open. Again I fell into a deep sleep. This time when I woke up (at least I felt I was awake) I was in a different place. This place was a house that was dark and scary. I discovered myself to be standing in the midst of the bedroom of the house where I grew up as a child.

This was an oblong bedroom that my parents, my sister and I shared together. My parents' bed was at one end of the room; and the bed my sister and I shared was at the opposite end of the room.

Since we did not have closets in the three-room house, we had to hang clothes on nails along aside the bedroom walls. Of course, in the dark these clothes resemble the appearances of hideous monsters. What a sight!

From my side of the bed, I could see into the living room. A window was directly in my eyesight. Needless to say, I was already jittery, frightened, and terrified when I first woke up. But there was something in my eye's view that made my heart stop ticking and my body petrified almost to a complete shutdown. I saw a thick, black, and hairy perhaps a worm going continuously around that living room window. I could not distinguish the head from the tail. It seemed to be joined as one enormous hairy creature. It appeared to be the size of my pillows on my bed. I rubbed and blinked my eyes to make sure

I was awake and not dreaming. I was awake. This phantom, this fictitious image could have been nothing but an optical illusion that was playing tricks on my mind. I mindfully observed with an attentive eye, hoping this thing would go away. As I became profoundly inquisitive the hairy creature seem to grow larger. It sensed I was watching it. So I eased the covers over my head so only my eyes would be showing. It moved continuously and it never stopped. I just knew at any given moment that black hairy creature would leave that window and crawl into bed with my sister and I. My heart started beating again, and my pulse rate soared beyond the normal speed.

I grew impatient and weary. Neither my sister nor my mother woke up. They were fast asleep. My father was away. We needed protection. Somebody needs to be a hero. I could not help because I barely managed to change position in the bed. I was too afraid to move. When I did move, I was facing my sister.

As soon as I got comfortable, I raised up out of that bed. I saw flying white clothes gliding and soaring through the air. This was insane and impossible, but it was happening. I could not believe my eyes. My mouth fell open and I began to drool as I witness the unimaginable sights before my eyes. I looked over my shoulder searching for the black creature that encircled the window. It was still there.

And then I heard voices whispering and chattering. They were talking to me. I could not understand the language; then again I really didn't care. I was scared! I buried myself a little deeper down into the bed. The whispering continued for some time. Why haven't my mother and sister woken up by now? Can't they hear the whispering? I knew it was some sort of evil that was stirring in the air. And it all seemed to be aimed at me.

Nobody else in my family seemed to be distracted by this bizarre and uncanny schedule of events.

I wanted to scream; who would hear me? I felt lonely. I lay in silence while my eyes wondered from wall to wall observing all the dreadful sights in that long narrow bedroom. My mind racing to tell me to do this and to do that, but my body saying there is nothing I can do but lie here. My mouth became as dry as cotton.

I had made up my mind I was going to leave my bed and get into the bed with my mother. What good would that do? For me, it was a means of safety. At least my mind would be at ease. So I whispered to my sister and told her of the danger we were encountering. She could not believe her ears. She became timid and shook with fright.

Then I noticed something was different. The clothes were not flying, the black hairy creature at the window was gone, and the whispering had stop. Evil games of the dark world and I was not impressed. Did this evilness stop because my sister was awake? They were targeting me, right? I don't have a clue, but one thing for sure I wasn't going to stick around to find out.

My sister and I agreed on the count of three we would flee to safety to my mother's bed. We counted to three and we froze. We were so petrified with fear that our muscles resist the ability to move. So we tried again. This time my sister managed to escape. I tried to follow right behind her, but something grabbed hold of my foot. Like the suction of a vacuum cleaner it held me and would not let go. In slow motion I could feel myself reaching out to my sister for help. There was no sound only awkward and desperate movement for escape. I struggled, squirmed, pulled, tugged, and screamed like it was bloody murder. I finally tore away to safety and in one swift move; I dived into my mother's bed.

I could hear those whispers again, but this time I was able to acknowledge that which was being communicated to me. The whispers were squeaky and horrid sounds of laughter saying, "we will get you next time, you wait and see." Then there was the sound of a key entering the doorknob at the front door. That was my father coming home. POOF! My home was normal again.

I woke up to reality grasping the concept that this dream is a little too real for me. I hope I can finally go to sleep peacefully and not be carried away to—God knows what. I was relieved to be in my very own bed and to see that everything looked as it did when I fell asleep.

Destination

I glanced at the clock and noticed it hasn't been three hours since I first fell asleep. It appears I should have been sleeping for days. I think the excitement of these weird dreams have kept me going consciously and subconsciously. I am almost to the point where I am afraid to fall asleep again. I fear the unknown. And you can't handle anything that you don't know anything about. Trapped, thoughtless, and unable to defend or defeat the unexpected, I fear this.

I was talking to myself in a low monotone voice. I tried my best NOT to fall back to sleep because I wanted some peaceful sleep and not a dreadful nightmare. I was tossing and turning until I could not fight it any longer. As my body relaxed, my head would bob and jerk, as my eyelids became heavy. I gave in and fell into a deep tranquil sleep again.

I saw a white house in the country that was surrounded by woods. The beauty of nature, peacefulness and serenity that exists around that house intrigued me. So I made my way toward that house. This house reminds me of a fairy tale about a little cottage surrounded by a forest. I began to shout to see if anybody could hear me—nobody answered.

This is a picture perfect setting and I did not like the vibes I was beginning to experience. My heart was fluttering and my palms began to sweat. I took a deep breath and was hoping the big bad wolf or the wicked witch would not come from around the corner of the house.

I was curious to know who or what occupied that house. I turned the doorknob and crossed the threshold to find the atmosphere of the inside of the house was completely different than that of the outside of the house. As I walked further, the peaceful house transformed into some large gray cold concrete building. Not knowing what I may walk upon, I cautiously explored the room. I heard noises and I gazed to my left. I knew now that I had walked into hell! Before my eyes, I saw people moving spastically as if they were filled with madness. Everybody was in a hurry. I saw signs of distress, fear, and panic. The screams, moaning, and wailing were too bearable for my ears to hear.

Suddenly, there was a loud power blast as if an explosive bomb had gone off. The rooms were filled with smoke. As the air was clearing, I tried to find my way back out. I stumbled upon a room and discovered a very awful stinking smell. The smell of blood and death was in the air. A glimpse at the room nearest me caused me to fall to my knees. Human flesh and decaying bodies lay scattered about in the room. I became nauseated and vomited profusely. Large rats and maggots were having a field day feasting off the decayed matter. Disgusted by the sight, I quickly ran back out the door in search of fresh air.

I vomited again and again on my hands, feet, and clothes. My common sense, my intellectual thinking was spending like a blender inside my head. When I did completely come back to my senses, I thought about all the commotion that was going on in that house.

It occurred to me that these people were from another part of the world, like the Far East. Was I in the Far East? My curiosity got the best of me so I went back into the house (building). This time I had to cover my nose and mouth in order for me to breathe.

As I opened the door, I was almost stampeded by the crowd rushing out the door. "Where are they going in such a hurry," I asked myself? These people never noticed me standing at the door, but I noticed them. I could not understand what they were saying, but it doesn't take an idiot to see they were very terrified by something. I purposely tripped one young man. (I hope this person can understand English).

I asked the young man about what was going on. He had a puzzle look on his face. He panted as he tried to talk. He pointed toward the house and said the 'the Yellow Devil'. I shrugged my shoulders waiting for more details of this Yellow Devil. Constantly watching over his shoulder, he tried to elaborate about the Yellow Devil. It was a huge fierce powerful beast that roams the eastern part of the hemisphere of the world. I suggested just kill the beast. According to the young man, it was not that simple. Several attempts have been made to destroy this beast, but none were successful.

"This is the great beast of Satan. It's here to destroy and kill. It possesses your mind, soul, and heart if you let it. It entraps you and there is no escaping. That's what happened to us. We became trapped in this building. Yes it looks like a beautiful house on the outside. But once you are inside, you fall prey to this evil demon. The beast has the controlling power of every man that looks upon its face or places a foot upon its territories. The doors lock behind you and you can't get out. Evilness is brought upon the building then there is destruction among the people. It bellowed a ferocious outcry yielding a message saying, 'I rule and the earth shall be mine.' It was intended for us to be imprisoned in that building until we had completely destroyed one another. You are the key that unlocked the door to our freedom and salvation. You are an angel sent by God. Thank you so much. My people will show you their gratitude by the gifts that lay before you on the ground."

I looked on the ground there was something of everything lying before my eyes. I saw money, jewelry, clothes, dishes, shoes, bags, and so much more. The young man warned me to never look upon the face of the Yellow Devil; then he left very quickly with the rest of his people.

I was about to pick up all the gifts I had received, until I heard a thunderous roar. I said to myself, "I am sure that's not the great evil one?" I picked up my pace and moved a little faster. I was about to walk away when my internal instinct said, "look, but don't look." I slowly turned around. My eyes came in contact with a great demon the first I have ever seen in my life. I could not exactly describe the physical appearance of the beast. But the beast seems to be as huge as the house; (at least it appeared that way.) By now my sensory impulses were incapable of perceiving mental ideas to project visual images. My nerves were disturbed; they were blown into complete shock. Whatever life I had in my body at time had left me. It was like somebody had knocked the breath out of me because I could not breathe. I dropped everything I had gathered from the ground. I wanted to run, but could not move. My feet were fixated to the ground.

Rampaging and brutally, the Yellow Devil attacked the house. My eyes grew large with fear as I quivered watching the Yellow Devil strip the house down into splinters in a split second. It was looking for food. I understand now. The house was a storage place for food, and the people trapped inside were meals for the Yellow Devil. Thank God I came along when I did to save them.

The Yellow Devil was outraged because there were no people in that house for it to feast on. The beast looked up and noticed me. I squirmed, cried, and peed on myself at the thought of the Yellow Devil waiting to devour me. It's loud evil roar sounded and felt deadly like a sword piercing my heart. I ached from shaking so much.

And then it happened. My eyes met the eyes of the Yellow Devil. It seemed if that old devil could read my mind. I heard a voice in the background saying, "Remember not to look into the eyes of the Yellow Devil because you will be the next victim it hunts until it destroys you." Now he reminds me. It's too late. I could hear myself saying, "May the God in heaven who is the father of Abraham, Isaac, and Jacob protect me from this evilness until this beast is destroyed."

Multitudes of people were racing in my direction with all sorts of weapons in their hands. The battle was on! And I was standing in the midst of what was about to be a bloody massacre. I felt weak and then I fainted. When I came to, I felt like I was still in combat because of my defensive and hostile actions and my heavy breathing. I retaliated and defended until my actions came to a sudden halt. My weary bewildered mind became conscious of my surroundings. I was awake!

I held my breath and sat up in my bed dazed. I touched my pillow it was soaking wet and so was the bed. I myself was soaked as well. Sweat poured down along the sides of my temples and forehead. I was nervous and my palms were sweating. Aching with discomfort, my chest wall pounded continuously and my mind raced rapidly from the thoughts of the combat. I observed the room slowly then exhaustingly released my breath.

It was over and I was thankful that I did not have to see the Yellow Devil again. I thought my life was over. I had a thought that left me thinking the devil is just as close to us as it is far away. I knew I was safe in my own haven. I knew things of that nature I did not have to worry about, or did I? I gradually fell back onto my pillow looking up at the ceiling. That was the last thought I had before I fell sound asleep.

I jumped and became startled at the sound of glass breaking. The room was dark except for the gleam of moonlight that was shining through my window. Immediately, I wanted to jump up, but I couldn't. Instead, I lay quietly thinking for a moment before I ventured onto my next move.

I remember hearing a fast panting sound that was coming from somewhere within the room. I was like a dog with a keen sense of hearing trying to interpret the sound without having to get up. The sound was similar to that of desperate breathing or gasping for air.

The breathing stopped and I lost my pathway to finding the origin of that sound. I swallowed hard. Without moving a muscle of my petrified body, I found the origin of the breathing. There it was resting at the threshold of my bedroom, the devil himself. I could see the eyes mutating suddenly from a glowing yellow to that of hot red coals as it kept a hawk's eye directly at me.

I am the destined prey the beast is in search of. It found me and now it waits with anticipation to destroy me. But this cannot be; are my eyes deceiving me the Yellow Devil in my house? My heart sank and my petrified body was now a complete shutdown. "Oh Lord, why me? This can't be the result of my looking that beast into its eyes? That was only a dream," I said to myself. "I am glad the beast cannot see my eyes right now because they were hidden by my right arm resting across my forehead."

By now I was confused, frighten, upset, dumbfounded, speechless, nauseated, and just totally—I have no clues. I felt I was absolutely at the mercy of the Yellow Devil? I was not going to be like those people in that house. In my mind, I decided to commence an escape plan. First, I wanted to see if I could move my legs, but I could not. The beast growled and I changed my mind about moving ANY part of my body.

I am doomed. I the victimized prey will soon be breakfast for this horrific beast. Cleverly, the beast crept closer to my bed. I could sense its closeness because of its wild distinctive odor that stunk up my room as it moved. And the tone of the harsh breathing grew louder and louder. I suddenly felt this hot heavy breathing on my arm. I flinched and cautiously curled myself into a knot as hard as I could. I was hoping this would make me disappear. I sensed anger from this beast.

Unexpectedly, the enraged beast pounced upon me and began gnawing at my shoulder. I could foresee what was about to happen. I quickly grabbed a pillow to use as a barrier to obstruct the brutal acts that were about to take place by that savage beast. I was unable to move because I was pin down by the beast's enormous claws. Desperately, ripping the pillow to shreds, it clawed its way at me. The beast thirsted for my blood. It forcibly tried to sever my throat with its large front incisors as it reached for my jugular vein.

I don't know if it was from my being afraid or if my bodily organs were beginning to malfunction as I peed and defecated on myself. There was nothing I could do. Water filled my eyes and I could feel the tears trickling down my face. I could feel myself loosing to this evil beast, but I was not about to give up hope.

As the struggle continued between the beast and me, I noticed everything around me was moving in complete slow motion. The objects on my nightstand (Bible, glass of water, and a gold letter opener) fell onto my bed, but the alarm clock fell at the feet of the beast.

The beast had three paws resting on me while he wrestled the clock with the other paw. It was like he was trying to destroy the clock so that it would not alarm. "Does this alarm clock have an affect on the situation that is going on between the beast and me?" I asked myself. "This beast has enough sense to know that he has control of me as long as that clock does not alarm. OH MY GOD, PLEASE ALARM CLOCK!" I shouted before I knew it and the beast swung around and clawed me with a hard slap. The beast continued until it was satisfied that the alarm clock would not alarm.

My last hope was to pray real hard. What came to my mind at that time was the beast in Revelation. The purpose of the beast is to destroy the inhabitants of the earth. The beast would rule and the believers would worship it. Then I thought about Jesus hanging on the cross as I felt a sharp pain pierce my neck as blood dripped onto the sheets.

At once the pain ceased. The beast suddenly jerked away and roared like I never heard it roar before. It sounded like a deep wailing desperate cry for help or the cry of someone suffering immense agony. The roaring made my ears throb in great pain. I cried harder.

Not realizing I was holding the gold letter opener in my hand, I had unknowingly stabbed the beast.

As I purposely looked into the eyes of the beast and gasped for air one last time I mumbled, "I rebuke the beast in the name of Jesus Christ." Then I was out.

And then there was a period of silence. That silence was broken by the sound of the alarm clock going off. I woke to the sound of the alarm clock. That sound irritated me so I snatched up the clock and threw it. As the clock went sailing across the room, I began to view the room in slow motion. This is not the last thing I remembered. I remembered praying, the beast, and the noises. What happened? Where was the beast?

I examined my pillow it was not ripped to shreds. I examined my room it was still in one piece. I went to the bathroom to examine myself in the mirror there were no punctured wound marks in my neck or any place on my body. I sighed with relief and joy. I do recall hearing the sound of glass breaking so I inspected the entire house, but I did not find any broken glass. And of course, there were no signs of forced entry into my house. All windows and doors were locked. "How did that Yellow Beast get into my house? And where did it go?" I wrestled with this thought.

To put my mind at ease, I thoroughly searched the house once more to make sure I did not overlook anything. The house was as I had left it before I went to sleep with everything still in place. I was puzzled and scared. I took a deep breath and walked to the front door. Through the window in the door, I could see dawn approaching. I thought to myself, "I have had enough of this night. I have not had a wink of restful sleep only nightmares. First the orphanage, the childhood memories, and now this helper of Satan have been more than I can stand to bear. What else is next? I hate to even ask."

I opened the front door and I glared through the window of the storm door. I noticed something glistening in the grass on the front lawn. I moved slowly toward the glistening object to see what it was.

I gasped when I saw the object. It was the gold letter opener that lay on my nightstand. I thought to myself how did this get outside? The last time I remembered seeing this I was defending myself against the beast.

I picked up the gold letter opener and carried it back into the house. I cleaned it up and placed it back inside my Bible as if nothing had happened. I pulled the covers back on the bed to make sure there were no bloodstains on my sheets. They were clean. I smiled.

I got on my knees and started to pray. I was afraid to close my eyes fearing I might open them up to see something I did not want to see. When I finished praying, I slowly opened my eyes. The room, the whole house, and the world were filled with light. The sun was shining bright and the birds were chirping. I knew that God had saved me because I did my Christian duty to save those other people from that horrific beast. He heard my prayer and made the Yellow Devil vanish from my mind and hopefully my memory.

After all this, it dawned on me that I had gotten too busy and caught up in my daily life that I forgot to pray before I fell asleep. Tonight was the one chance I almost gave the devil to intercept into my life and to almost run me foolish throughout this whole conflicting night, he was in my home and my mind, but fortunately he was not in my heart. Now I am finally rid of that evil.

It doesn't matter who you are or where you are from; the devil is here to destroy. So be careful the devil maybe after you. He may come in the form of a man, animal, or he may just come into your dreams.

About the Author

Born in 1963 in a little community called Bolivar, Tennessee. I began writing as early as the fourth grade in Toone Elementary School. I attended Tennessee State University and Jackson State Community College. It wasn't until after high school that I really became intoned with my writing. I am a divorced mother with two boys. I work as an Admission Specialist at a hospital in Jackson, Tennessee.

0-595-23379-1

Printed in the United States
52746LVS00002B/285